AGAINST THE WIND

Cowgirls in Time Romance Series

A Chill Wind

Wind Beneath My Wings

Against the Wind

AGAINST THE WIND

Erica Einhorn

Ralston Store Publishing
P.O. Box 1684
Prescott, Arizona 86302

ISBN 978-1-938322-25-9

Professionally and lovingly edited by:
Jennifer Hope
www.MesaVerdeMediaServices.com

Printed in the USA.

Dedicated to the one I love

CHAPTER ONE

WHAT A GLORIOUS day to be alive on this earth! The sun streamed through the window, and Madison could see the brilliant blue sky with the mountains in the background. She stretched, yawned, and hugged herself in gratitude for how lucky she was. Walking around the different rooms in the big house, she marveled that it was all hers. Well, not exactly hers. The house still belonged to her Aunt Jenna who was now living happily ever after in the old Red Bluff. Jenna and her husband, Josiah, were content and settled in the nineteenth century. They only came back to the house occasionally, for dinner out or supplies—supplies they couldn't get back there—like batteries and Rocky Road ice cream.

Meanwhile, the house was all hers. She walked into the kitchen and started the coffee. Then she took the cinnamon roll out of the refrigerator. Putting it in the microwave, she glanced into the front room. Her mother would not approve. Kat, as everyone called her, was a nurse practitioner who kept a strict diet. No wheat, no sugar, no beef unless grass fed—Madison couldn't even remember all of her mother's diet restrictions. But she was not interested in following that regimen, so she removed the warm roll, inhaled the cinnamon-ness of it, took a bite, and closed her eyes. Best cinnamon rolls in town!

As she walked by the side of the refrigerator on her way to get a coffee cup, she frowned. It was almost Father's Day. Madison hated Father's Day. Her father, Billy, had died in the middle east when she was a baby. She never had the opportunity to call him "Daddy." Whenever her mother spoke of him, she spoke of "Billy," so that's how Madison thought of him. When she was a little girl, she'd ask her mother endless questions about him. So she thought she had the sense of him, the feel of him, in her head. But there was an empty place in her heart that would never be filled.

When she was in school, she dreaded all the Father's Days and the Father/Daughter dances. In art class, while everyone else made Father's Days gifts for their fathers, Madison would deliberately do something bad to get sent to the principal's office. Although she was a model student the rest of the time, no one ever figured out why she'd always misbehave right before Father's Day. Whatever punishment she received was always better than having to create a Father's Day card for a father who didn't exist. She suspected that her mother knew—although she had never said anything about it—and Madison never admitted it. Sure, there were other kids in school whose parents were divorced—plenty of them. But there was a drastic difference between an absentee father and no father at all. In the small elementary school that she had attended, there was one boy who had also lost his father. That didn't diminish the pain, though.

Madison tightened her lips and frowned. She hated that her mother didn't use Billy's last name. Kat said it was easier that way and eventually Madison would understand. But at twenty-one years old, Madison still did not understand. She used his last name with pride and walked tall. Madison always walked tall.

CHAPTER TWO

MOANING. SOMEONE WAS moaning, and it was keeping him awake. How could he fall back to sleep with that blasted noise? And he was freezing. His whole body shook with the chills. As Zack struggled to open his eyes, the morning light filtered through the curtains and the moaning stopped. Then he realized the moaning had been coming from him.

The room swirled around him. He closed his eyes and took a deep breath. It was morning, and he had a job to do. Opening his eyes again, he waited for the room to still. Cradling his arm, he swung his legs over the side of the bed. When the room swirled again, he swayed and fell backward onto the bed. This time he didn't fight it. The moaning started again, and the pain was intense. It had been getting steadily worse for the past few days, but this was the worst. How could he work when his arm hurt this bad? Zack didn't remember Sheriff Josiah complaining that his arm hurt this bad when he was shot.

He didn't know how much time had passed before he heard a knock at the door. "Zack? Zack!" More knocking. Zack tried to call out, but his voice came out as a squeak. Then the door opened.

Sarah rushed to the side of his bed, lightly brushing his arm as she put her hand on his forehead. He tried to focus his eyes on her. "Zack, are you all right? Oh, no! You're burning up! Is your arm all right?"

"Ow! Don't touch it! It hurts!" Although Sarah had barely touched his arm, it hurt too badly to let anyone near it.

"Zack, I need to put my hand on your arm," said Sarah.

"No, it hurts," said Zack, as he rolled away from her.

"Zack, I need to do this. Now please let me. I won't hurt it. I'll just put my palm on your arm. I need to touch it. Please."

Zack rolled back toward her and said, "Be gentle."

Sarah gently placed her hand on his arm, barely touching the skin. Then she put her hand on his forehead again. "Zack, you're burning up with fever, and your arm is hot." She pushed up his sleeve to look at the arm. "It's a good thing that there are no red streaks, so you don't have blood poisoning. Yet. You need to see a doctor. Now."

"No. All he'll do is bleed me. I don't want to be bled. I'll be fine."

"I'm going to get Matthew." Sarah disappeared out the door.

Zack tried to sit up, but couldn't. He wanted to use Sarah's toilet. It wasn't Sarah's anymore. Since she had married and moved in with Matthew, Zack had gotten her room and her toilet. Sarah called it a composting toilet. He didn't care what it was called. It was convenient, and he didn't have to go outside to the necessary.

But he was too weak to even sit up. He didn't dare try to walk across the room. Lost in his own thoughts, the sound of the door opening and Matthew bursting in, followed by Sarah, surprised Zack.

"Sarah says you're sick," said Matthew. "How do you feel?"

"I'm fine," said Zack, as he tried to sit up, failed, and fell backward onto the bed. "But can you help me use the toilet, please?"

"He needs a doctor, Matthew. It's serious."

"I don't want a doctor. He'll just bleed me again, and it didn't help before."

"Zack's right," said Matthew. "The doctor will just bleed him."

"Matthew, I want to take him to the *other* doctor," said Sarah.

"There is no other doctor, Sarah. Doc Mercer is the only doctor in town," said Matthew.

"No, Matthew, I mean the *other* doctor," said Sarah, as she raised her eyebrows. Zack had no idea what other doctor she meant or why she raised her eyebrows at Matthew. But he intended on staying right there until he felt better.

"Oh!" said Matthew, stepping away from the bed and looking from Zack to Sarah and back to Zack again. "We couldn't. Oh, no, that's not possible. I mean, he doesn't know."

"Could you two argue someplace else? Know what? What don't I know? Matthew, can you help me to the toilet?"

"His arm is *infected*, Matthew. Seriously infected. He needs to see a doctor. A *real* doctor. And I'm going to take him—no matter what you or Zack say. He's going!"

Sarah stomped out the door.

Matthew helped him up from the bed and asked, "Zack, why are you still in your clothes?"

"I didn't feel good enough last night to get 'em off."

When Matthew helped him back into bed after he used the toilet, Zack realized how weak he was. He could barely stand up without Matthew's help. Still, he didn't want to see any doctor. All Doc Mercer had done for him when he saw him last week was bleed him. It didn't help then, and it wouldn't help now. Zack knew he needed something else, but he didn't know what. He hoped that with a little more rest, he'd feel more like his old self.

The door opened, and Sarah walked in. "It's ready. Help me get him down the stairs."

"I'm not going anywhere, Sarah." Zack lay back down on the bed.

"He doesn't want to," said Matthew.

Sarah stomped back over to the bed and gently lifted Zack's arm. "Feel that arm, Matthew. Then put your hand on his forehead. He's hot! His arm is hot! The boy is sick and needs a doctor—a real doctor. He's not going to get that here. He needs to go *there.*"

Zack didn't know where *there* was, but he wasn't going anywhere. He allowed Matthew to touch his arm, and then he pulled it back, cradled it, and turned his back on Matthew and Sarah. "I'm not going."

"But he doesn't know anything about, um, *there,*" said Matthew.

"It doesn't matter. He needs to go. Besides, he would have found out eventually from Madison," said Sarah.

"Madison," said Zack, turning around. "You're taking me where Madison is?" Zack liked Madison. He had met her a time or two before and had enjoyed talking to her.

And she was pretty.

"Yes, Zack. Come with me, now, and you'll see Madison," said Sarah.

"Okay." Zack struggled to get up, and Matthew helped him.

"Let's get him downstairs," said Sarah. "Easy now."

As they started walking him through the door, Zack said, "Wait! My book! I want my book." Matthew propped him in the doorway and walked to get his book from the bedside table. He held it up so Sarah could see.

"*Purdon's Digest of Laws of Pennsylvania*? This isn't Pennsylvania. Why are you reading that?" asked Sarah.

"He wants to be a lawyer," said Matthew.

"I read everything I can about the law," said Zack.

With Sarah on one side of him and Matthew on the other, they helped him downstairs. He realized even more how weak he was. Without them, he would have toppled down the stairs. They helped him walk through the saloon and out the front doors. A horse and a narrow wagon waited outside.

"Help me get him in the back," said Sarah.

After a few attempts, they were able to get him into the back of the wagon. He lay down on the empty grain sacks, with a full bag for a pillow.

"See how nice Ezra made it for you, Zack?" asked Sarah. Ezra ran the livery stable where Sarah had rented the horse and wagon. Dancer, Sarah's horse, wouldn't pull a wagon if you paid him, thought Zack.

"Matthew, can you bring him a blanket?" asked Sarah.

While Matthew walked back into the saloon to get a blanket from upstairs, Zack relaxed onto the empty grain sacks. Walking down the stairs and climbing into the wagon had exhausted him. He had no idea how he would get out of the wagon. How far away did Madison live, anyway?

Matthew came back and wrapped Zack in the blanket. It felt good, but a little tight around his sore arm, so he pulled the arm out and put it on top of the blanket. "I'm ready," said Zack. "I guess." He closed his eyes and listened to the conversation between Matthew and Sarah, although he didn't understand it.

"Are you sure you want to do this, Sarah? We can find another way. Maybe have Kat come here," said Matthew.

"No, Matthew. I'm afraid it's really bad, and there's no time. I don't want him to lose his arm."

"Lose my arm?" asked Zack. "It's not going anywhere." He brought it back under the blanket, just in case.

"Okay, Sarah, if you have to. When will you come home?" asked Matthew.

"After I get him taken care of. I'll have to call Kat and see if he needs to go to a hospital."

"I love you, Sarah. Take care of Zack," said Matthew.

"Love you, too, Matthew," said Sarah.

Zack heard them kiss, and then he fell into a restless sleep.

CHAPTER THREE

ZACK AWOKE WITH a start. He realized he was riding in a wagon—he could feel the wheels rolling beneath him—but he didn't know why. When he touched his sore arm, he cried out in pain. It had gotten worse. Now he remembered. Sarah was taking him someplace to see a doctor—someplace where Madison was.

"Zack, are you okay?" asked Sarah.

"Not exactly okay, but I'm still here," said Zack.

"Zack, I need to talk to you about something important. Are you alert enough to listen to me?"

"Yeah, but where are we, Sarah? This looks like a cave."

"It *is* a cave, Zack. It is a cave that leads to the future. Jenna, Ryan, Granny, and I all come from the future."

"And Madison? Does she come from the future, too?" asked Zack.

"Yes, and Madison, too."

"The future? What do you mean?"

"What year is it, Zack?"

"1870."

"When we come out of the cave in another minute,

we will be in 2014."

"2014? How is that possible? I think you're trying to bamboozle me, Sarah."

"Bamboozle? You mean kid you? No. And to answer your question, none of us know how it's possible, but we have all been going back and forth for months now."

"Has Matthew been there?"

"Yes, Matthew has been there. He didn't want to go, but I convinced him that he needed to. You know when Matthew asks if you can handle the saloon for an evening or two? We come here to eat. Matthew likes Thai food," said Sarah and laughed.

"Tie? What do you mean?"

"Too complicated to explain. You'll be here for a while, so you'll find out soon enough."

"How long will I have to stay? I mean, how long can I stay? I might like this future of yours. Besides helping Matthew out, there's not a lot to keep me in Red Bluff."

"Oh, no, you don't, Zack. You will go to the doctor, and when you're well enough, you will return to the old Red Bluff."

They emerged from the cave into the bright sunlight. It hurt Zack's eyes, so he closed them. "Tell me more about the future, Sarah. I want to hear, but I need to rest now."

"We'll get you fixed up right away, Zack, and you'll feel much better."

"Tell me more, Sarah."

"Okay, well, remember Hilary Clinton, the rustler?"

"Sure. Sheriff Josiah caught him."

"Yes, but it was Jenna who figured out who he was. Do you know how she figured it out?"

"No," said Zack.

"Because Hillary Clinton is a former president's wife. She was also a senator and secretary of state."

"Secretary what?"

"Zack, are you okay? Do you want me to keep quiet now so you can sleep?"

"No, keep talking. I want to hear more about your future."

Sarah continued talking about cars, trucks, cell phones, skyscrapers, and airplanes. Zack fell asleep sometime after she described the machines that flew through the sky.

CHAPTER FOUR

AFTER MADISON FINISHED savoring her last sip of coffee, she looked out the window again at the mountains and the bright blue sky. Today might be a good day for a long ride into the mountains. She could pack a lunch and make a picnic out of it. Closing the front door behind her, she walked out to the barn. Since each stall had its own automatic hay feeder, besides a quick check to see if they were all functioning properly, she didn't need to spend much time in the barn. But she loved it—loved being around the horses and loved the "horse air"—the pleasant aromas that accompanied the horses' environment. Sometimes as she brushed her horse, she would stop, put her cheek against his neck, and just inhale the horsey perfume. There was nothing better.

There were only a couple of horses in the barn nowadays. Aunt Jenna took her horse when she moved to the old Red Bluff, and Uncle Ryan did as well, as did Sarah when she moved there, and Granny—who was Madison's great-grandmother, but everyone called her Granny—took Jenna's horse, Dolly, when she moved there. So the only horses in the barn now were her mother's horse, Paisley, and Madison's horse, Chaco. Paisley was a leopard appaloosa—an older and well-behaved mare that her mother had had for years and years.

Madison's horse, Chaco, had begun as a 4-H project. He had been a three-year old mustang, fresh off the range. Chaco was a brown and white pinto, with a bald face, three black socks, black mane and tail, and one blue eye. He had only been handled long enough to scare the dickens out of him when they forced him into a squeeze chamber to freeze-brand him and anesthetize him so they could geld him. It wasn't a great beginning between him and humans. When Madison first got him, she'd sit at the side of his corral with a handful of hay. It took patience—and hours—but eventually he would eat the hay from her hands. At first reluctantly, and later he'd take it from her with more enthusiasm.

From there, she would hold the hay in one hand and slowly bring her other hand toward the side of his face. It took more time and more patience, but after a while he relished her touches. She continued working with him every day, and their bond grew stronger. The real breakthrough came one day when Madison was lying out in the middle of the pasture after having a fight with her mother. Chaco came out of nowhere, sniffed her once or twice, and then lay down beside her with his head on her stomach. From then on, they were inseparable.

The rest of his training went slowly, because Madison didn't want to push him. First, she'd lean over his back until he was used to the feel of her weight on him. Then she'd push herself onto his back and immediately off again. Next, she'd stay up there for a few seconds and gradually increase the time. When she finally got around to riding him, he didn't buck even once. Well, except the time she put the saddle on him wrong, and it pinched him. She went flying that day, but Chaco didn't hold it against her. These days, both preferred to ride bareback, although Chaco would tolerate a saddle if it didn't pinch him.

Chaco and Paisley both nickered as she approached. Madison stroked Paisley's face and then walked into Chaco's stall to hug him. She moved her hand along his back and legs, getting some dust off.

"Chaco, would you like to go on a long ride today? We haven't done that for a while. It will be fun, huh?" In response, Chaco turned around, grabbed a mouthful of hay, and began munching. "Is that a no, then?" Madison patted the horse on his rump. She sighed. "Well, I guess I don't much feel like going either." After one last stroke on his neck, Madison locked up the stall and walked back to the house.

Chaco was usually as eager to go for a ride as she was, so when he acted like he didn't want to go, Madison listened. But she wasn't really disappointed. Lately riding alone had gotten her down. She enjoyed riding and had always cherished the time alone on the trail with Chaco, but it had begun to feel like something was missing. Like she was missing something essential to her.

Her whole life had started to feel like that. Although she loved college and loved what she was studying, something felt missing. During the three years she had spent in college so far, she had made a conscious effort not to get involved with any men. Her studies were important to her, and she didn't want anything to upset that delicate balance. Now she wondered if maybe she had been missing an important part of college life. A boyfriend.

Not that she had even met anyone with whom she

might consider a relationship. Well, except Zack. But he was from the old Red Bluff. Madison wasn't like Aunt Jenna or Sarah or Uncle Ryan, or even Granny for that matter. She had no desire to live in the nineteenth century. To use a cliche, it was a fun place to visit, but she wouldn't want to live there. Madison considered herself a woman of the twenty-first century. She came equipped with her iPhone, her iPad, her laptop computer—and she wasn't willing to give any of that up. No. She liked living in the "new" Red Bluff, and she knew she would stay here. So a relationship with Zack was not even worth considering.

Madison finished the vacuuming, cleaned up the kitchen, and started the dishwasher. She felt she had to keep the house really clean, because she never knew when anyone was going to drop in. It wasn't like Aunt Jenna or Sarah could call and let her know. They hadn't figured out yet how to communicate from one century to another—not that they ever would—but it was something to think about.

Walking back into the living room, she plopped down on the sofa. This house was so big. Although she did have people visit quite regularly, it still felt huge for just her. When her Aunt Jenna had first asked if she wanted to live in the house, she had jumped at the chance. At the time, she was sharing a two-bedroom apartment with two other women. Other people had "offered" to share the house, but since all Madison had to pay was utilities, she didn't need anyone. And after the cramped apartment, living alone for a while sounded great. Now, it was starting to feel lonely. It was a big house. She wanted someone to talk to.

As she sat there, pondering the possibilities and feeling

lonely, she propped her feet up on the coffee table. She leaned back and sighed. Madison needed a change in her life, a big change. She needed someone to talk to, someone to share her life with, someone to talk over her studies. But who would that be? Then the doorbell rang. And rang again and again. Six times in quick succession, like someone was in a hurry. Madison rushed to answer the door.

CHAPTER FIVE

"SARAH! WHAT'S GOING on? You know you can just walk in."

"Madison! Hurry! Help me get Zack into the house."

"Zack?" said Madison, concerned. She followed Sarah out to the horse and wagon parked in front of the house. Zack was lying in the back, under a blanket, with his head on a sack of grain, and looking pale. "Is he okay?"

Zack moaned, opened his eyes, and looked at Madison. "Mmmm. I'll be okay. Would you believe that Sarah's been telling me tall tales about coming to the future? I think she wanted to keep my mind occupied so the arm wouldn't hurt so much. How are you, Madison?"

He tried to sit up by himself, but couldn't do it with just his one good arm. Sarah and Madison helped him to sit up, and then helped him out of the wagon and into the house.

When they got him seated on the couch, Madison said, "What happened? Why did you bring him here?"

"You know he got shot, right? When all the men came to rescue me? Anyway, his arm is infected, *very* infected. I wanted Kat to look at it. He might need to go to a hospital. I'll call her now." Sarah pulled the cell phone out of her pocket, while Madison stroked the hair out of Zack's face. Madison's cell phone rang.

"Hello?"

"Oh, Madison!" Sarah hung up the phone.

"Oh, we switched phones and numbers! Let me call her." As Madison moved her fingers across the iPhone, she looked up quickly and said, "Mom didn't like the iPhone, so we traded." Then she put the phone by her ear. "Hi, Mom. Listen, Sarah is here. She just brought Zack. . . . Yes, he's here now. Sarah says his arm is really infected and that he might need to go to the hospital. She wanted you to look at it. . . . Do what? . . . Oh, okay."

Madison turned her attention to Zack. "Mom says I need to look at your arm and feel it." When Zack held his arm protectively, Madison said, "I won't do anything to hurt you. I'll just put my hand on it gently and look."

"Oh, yeah, Mom, it's really hot," Madison said into the iPhone. "There is a lot of redness, but no streaks. . . . Yes, I'll tell her. . . . Okay, see you soon." Madison put the phone back into her pocket.

"What was that you were talking into?" asked Zack. Then, looking around the room and pointing to the television and the stereo, he asked, "And what's that? And that?"

Sarah and Madison both laughed. "Sarah, Mom said that you got him here just in time. Then she said some expletives about Doc Mercer, and said she might have to move back there just to take care of the people she loves!" Then, to Zack, she said, "Zack, Sarah wasn't kidding about bringing you to the future. The year is

2014. Welcome! I talked on my iPhone," she pointed across the room, "and that is called a television, I'll show it to you later, and that over there is a stereo that plays music. You'll like that. I think you'll like this future, Zack. I've been to your world, now welcome to mine! Oh! And wait until you see the kitchen! And the bathroom! You have all kinds of cool things in store for you in my world!"

"Can I see your iPhone thing?" asked Zack.

As Madison reached into her pocket to pull out her iPhone, Sarah put her hand on Zack's forehead and said, "Did she say how soon she'd be here?"

"Don't worry, Sarah. Mom knows that it's serious. She'll be here in fifteen minutes. She'll fix Zack right up!" Madison sat beside Zack on the couch, and when she leaned over to show him the phone, he screamed.

"Ow! My arm!"

"Oh, sorry, Zack. I'll sit on the other side of you." Madison moved to his other side. "Here. Let me show you how it works." A second later, Sarah's phone rang. "Sarah, will you go into the other room so Zack can talk to you?"

"He can talk to me here. I'm too worried about him to leave him alone."

"He's not alone. I'm with him, and Mom will be here in a minute. Come on, this will give you something to do so you won't worry so much."

Sarah sighed and walked into the other room, holding her cell phone to her ear. "Here, Zack," said Madison. "Hold it a little away from your ear, though. That's what my mom keeps telling me, anyway."

Zack held the phone close to his ear. "Sarah?" Then his face lit up, and he said, "I can hear you! I can hear you! What did you call this, Madison, cool? That's so cool!"

Madison laughed. "We'll make a twenty-first-century man out of you, yet, Zack!" She took the phone back from Zack. "Sarah, thank you." Then she held it up for Zack and showed him some of her favorite apps.

She was hoping to make him forget about the pain in his arm, and she hoped that her mother would arrive soon. Although she didn't show it, Madison felt as worried as Sarah was. The wound on Zack's arm looked terrible. She hoped her mother was right and that Zack wouldn't need to go to the hospital. And the arm looked so bad, swollen and all, that she hoped he wouldn't lose it. How would he get along in the nineteenth century with just one arm? Madison hoped that her mother could fix him up, and it wouldn't come to him losing an arm.

CHAPTER SIX

As Sarah paced back and forth, looking at her watch every few steps, Zack tried to put *her* concern out of *his* mind. She was really worried—which worried Zack. Even Madison, who tried to hide it by showing him all the cool, new things in this century, looked worried. Whatever the challenge of his illness, Zack felt confident that he could handle it. That's the kind of man he was. He handled whatever was put before him, and he handled it well. What was the worst that could happen? Lose his arm? He could handle it. Have the illness kill him? He could see his father and mother again. Nothing was too much for him.

At the same time, he knew when to back down, and he wasn't afraid to do that, either. When those men in Matthew's saloon, where he worked, made fun of him for being Indian, he ignored it. What else could he do? Even if he could get them to stop, there would be more men coming in who called him the same names. No, better to just ignore it and not let it bother him. It did bother him on some level—he knew that. But if he let those men know that it bothered him, it would make it that much worse.

That reminded him of the time when Sarah had stood up for him. When the man started calling Zack names, Sarah had calmly walked over to him and poured a bottle of whiskey in the guy's lap. Zack felt good that Sarah had cared enough about him to do that. But he also felt guilty about it.

That man, who was dead now, turned out to be one of the scalawags who kidnapped Sarah. Then, several men, including Zack, accompanied Sheriff Josiah to rescue Sarah. That's how Zack had ended up with a gunshot wound in his arm. He had gone to defend Sarah, as she had defended him, and he was proud of that. Still, a part of him wondered if maybe those men never would have kidnapped Sarah if she hadn't stood up for Zack. Sarah and Matthew both told him it would have happened anyway, but Zack couldn't get it out of his mind. And it made him that much more grateful that Sarah worried about him now. She obviously wasn't wrathy at him about it.

"And check this out, Zack," said Madison, disturbing his thoughts. "This is the television. See, this is the remote control, and you can change channels from here."

Madison put the device in his hands and showed him what buttons to press. Zack was so engrossed with changing the channels and looking at all the different images on the screen, it surprised him when he found Madison's mother, Kat, standing in front of him with a medicine bag in her hand.

"Madison! Turn that thing off! I need to get to work!" said Kat.

Zack handed the remote to Madison and said, "Hallo." He had met Kat once or twice before, but had never talked with her.

When the room was quiet, Kat said, "Let me see your arm, Zack. I'll take care of you."

"Is he going to be all right, Kat?" asked Sarah.

"Give me a minute to examine him, Sarah. But I can tell you right now that he was lucky you brought him right in. See these red marks around the wound? Next step is blood poisoning." Kat reached into her medicine bag, retrieved a thermometer, and quickly ran it across Zack's forehead.

"What was that?" asked Zack.

"A thermometer. You have a high fever. One hundred two degrees. I bet you've had the chills all day."

"Yeah, I've been cold. How does that thing know that I have a fever?"

"It's called a temporal artery thermometer. It works very well. Okay, Zack, take off your pants and roll over." And to Sarah and Madison, she said, "Ladies, leave the room and give Zack a moment of privacy so I can give him a penicillin shot."

"What's a penicillin shot?" asked Zack.

"I'm going to stick a needle in your bum and put some medicine in it."

"No! It sounds worse than getting my blood let!"

"You'll feel a lot better afterward, Zack," said Kat. "I guarantee it. A few hours from now, you'll be thanking me. But it will hurt a little."

"Are you a doctor?"

"No. I'm what's called a nurse practitioner. I can do much of what a doctor does, but not all—I can't do surgeries or anything—and I don't have the extensive education that a doctor does. Although, I *do* have more education than that Doc Mercer of yours. Did he wash his hands before he worked on you?"

"No. Ow! That hurts!"

"It's over now. Pull up your pants and let me work on your wound."

"What does washing your hands have to do with anything?" asked Zack.

"Hold on, Zack." Louder, she said, "Madison! Bring me some clean towels!"

Madison, followed by Sarah, walked back into the room carrying two large towels. Kat put them under Zack's arm.

"Let's see now. Washing hands gets rid of something called germs, which cause disease. That won't be widely known in your time for a few more years. Zack, the swelling and the pain should go down when the penicillin kicks in. You'll feel better after that. This might hurt while I clean out the wound."

"Is he going to be all right?" asked Sarah. "Does he need to go to the hospital?"

"No, he'll be fine. I'll need to come by and check on him every day for a few days," said Kat. "To make sure everything is healing. If the penicillin doesn't work for some reason, there would be a chance he would have to go to a hospital. But since he has never had penicillin before, there should be no problem."

"When can he go back to his own time?" asked Sarah.

"Like I said, I have to check on him regularly for the next few days. I'd say a week would be safe—if everything is healing properly."

"A week, wow," said Sarah.

"You don't need to stay with him, Sarah. You can go back. Madison and I can take care of him. He'll be fine here."

"Oh, okay. I'll be back in a week to pick him up."

"You don't need to do that, Sarah. In a week when he can ride a horse, Madison or I can take him back."

Sarah walked up to Zack and put her hand on his shoulder. "You'll be taken good care of here, Zack. Are you okay with staying?"

Zack gave a quick glance in Madison's direction and smiled. "Sure. I'll be fine here."

Sarah kissed him on the forehead and turned to walk toward the front door. "Kat, thanks for coming right over. Madison, thanks for everything."

"No problem, Sarah," said Madison.

"No worries, Sarah," said Kat. "It just makes me think that I need to move back there so this doesn't happen again because of that inept doctor. You did exactly right by immediately bringing him here. He might have died if you hadn't. Another day or two, and this could have turned into sepsis. You saved his life, Sarah."

Sarah winked at Zack. "I guess that makes us even, Zack." To the others, she added, "He got that bullet wound from saving my life. Bye, everybody."

"Sarah! Wait! My book!" said Zack.

"Oh, yes. It's in the wagon. I have no idea why you'd be reading about Pennsylvania law, Zack, but I'll bring it in."

CHAPTER SEVEN

HAD MADISON HEARD right? Did Sarah say the book was a *law* book? Before she had a chance to absorb that, her mother interrupted her thoughts.

"Madison, I need you to pick up this prescription. Zack, what's your last name?"

"Murphy."

Kat finished scribbling out the prescription and handed the paper to Madison. "There you go."

"Be right back, Mom. See ya, Zack. Mom will take good care of you."

Madison skipped out through the door and closed it behind her. Her mind raced so fast, she couldn't keep up with the thoughts. Zack was into *the law*? If that were true, they could have long discussions about it. Maybe argue both sides of a case for practice and study together. Maybe he could even be her roommate!

Oh, wait. She realized she had gotten carried away. Zack didn't even live in her century. And why would he even want to with all the pollution and the crime and everything else that was wrong with the twenty-first century? Madison, having lived with it all her life, only focused on the good things about this century. But Zack, who had first-hand knowledge of the past—who lived in the past—would never want to live here in her world.

Madison sighed. It was a pleasant fantasy and would have made a wonderful reality. A man who she already felt attracted to and who was interested in the same subject she was *and* who would live with her and be her roommate. It was the kind of win-win situation that dreams were made of. She knew better than that. Madison prided herself on being grounded in reality.

She had learned about reality in a roundabout way from her mother. Although Madison's father, Billy, had died when she was a baby, her mother believed he was coming home. And it wasn't that he was missing in action—he had been *killed* in action. Granted, there was nothing identifiable in the casket when he "came home," but others had seen it happen and testified that the car bomb that exploded at his post had killed him. Still, her mother hoped it was all a mistake and that he would come home to her. She went on hoping for enough years that Madison had been old enough to remember. Even as young as she was, Madison knew he wasn't coming home. Billy had come to her in dreams and told her that he wasn't coming home, but he would always be with her.

Still, knowing that he was always with her, but not having him there with her, felt very different. As a girl, she longed for her mother to remarry so she could have a father. But even after her mother finally gave up hope of Billy returning from the dead, she had that go-nowhere-crush on Nick, who was her Uncle Ryan's best friend. Madison always thought Nick was a jerk and hoped nothing would happen. In her mind, Nick was *not* "Daddy" material. That crush faded, too, after a while, and her mother had become devoted to her work and reconciled to living alone.

It made Madison sad that her mother didn't have someone to love. And Madison didn't want that to happen to her as well, but she was only twenty-one years old and had plenty of time. Even if it didn't work out with Zack, she had plenty of time to find someone else. Wait! She had to get Zack out of her mind. She didn't even know if it was really a law book that he was reading. Maybe it was a novel *about* law—which would mean nothing. Plenty of people read novels about lawyers, but had no real interest in the law or in becoming lawyers.

Besides, she had only talked to him a couple of times. She knew hardly anything about him. What could they have in common, anyway? Madison shook her head and smiled to herself. Girl, you need to get out more. Meet people, find a boyfriend, stop being so isolated with your schoolwork. She would start her summer job in a few days, and that would be good exposure for her. Maybe she'd meet someone there. Someone perfect.

After she got the prescription filled, she stepped back into the car and headed home. Zack was a nice boy and all, but thinking about a relationship with him wasn't realistic. Well, at least not now, anyway. Her attraction to him was merely that he was cute, with his dark hair and dark eyes. And different. How could he not be different being a boy from more than a hundred years in the past? Of course he was different. That was part of her attraction to him. She realized that.

Now he would be staying at her home for at least a week while he recovered. That was her chance to get to know him, find out more about him, and discover if there was any reality to her fantasy. Of course, once she started her job, she couldn't spend that much time with him. And maybe he'd recover quickly enough that her mother would let him go home before the week was out. Whatever was in store for her and Zack, she knew that at least for now, it was out of her control.

CHAPTER EIGHT

ZACK LAY BACK and rested on the pillow. He had promised Kat that he would take it easy. She said that he couldn't work hard and expect his arm to heal. But he couldn't help it—at least not when he was back in his own time. It was his job to help Matthew, and he took that responsibility seriously. After all, Matthew had taken him in when nobody else would. After Zack's father died, Zack had no one in the world he could count on. Eliza and Samuel, who owned the hotel, had given him a room for a while. But it was harming their income, so he knew he couldn't stay there. Then Matthew moved to town and bought the saloon. He said that if Zack helped him out, he could have free room and board. That was five years ago, and he had been living in the same place as Matthew since then. Well, until Matthew married Sarah, and then Zack moved out and stayed in the room that Sarah had occupied before they were married.

But now, here in *this* century, he had no responsibilities. Kat had said the house belonged to her sister, to Jenna, and that Zack was welcome to stay as long as he needed to. Zack knew Jenna. She had moved to Red Bluff several months before and had married Sheriff Josiah. Of course, Zack hadn't known that Jenna had moved from the future into the past to be with the man she loved. So had Sarah. And so had Granny.

Zack didn't understand that. Why would anyone leave *this* wonderful place of new inventions and opportunities for the limitations of his time? No, he didn't understand that at all. He had been in the future for less than a day, and he already didn't want to leave. Did he have to go back? Would it upset something in history if he stayed in the future? No, if that were true, then Jenna, Sarah, and Granny couldn't have moved to the past. Although, maybe it just went one way. Someone could move to the past, but they couldn't move to the future. That would make sense because they hadn't done anything in the past that wouldn't get done if they weren't there. But what if someone from the future did something in the past to change the past? It felt so confusing. He still hardly believed it himself. Another time, more than a century in the future. And here he was, lying in bed in the future. It hardly seemed possible.

If the thought crossed his mind that they were trying to hornswoggle him, it passed quickly. It was one thing for Sarah to tell him about this future time while he was riding in the back of a horse-drawn cart. It was something else to see the iPhone-thing and the television in action. Those were too remarkable to be products of his time.

Not to mention the bathroom that Kat had shown him before she left. There was a bathtub in it, but the room's primary purpose was to relieve yourself. It was even more convenient than the composting toilet that Sarah had brought into his life. He still couldn't get over how the water swirled around after you pushed on that little handle. After Kat had left him alone in the house, he had steadied himself with his hand on the wall and had gone back into the bathroom just to watch the water go down. He pressed the handle again and again so he could watch it. When he finally climbed back into bed, exhausted, he felt satisfied.

After Madison had left, Kat had carefully cleaned his wound, cursing Doc Mercer the whole time. She said the wound probably wouldn't have gotten infected if Doc Mercer had observed basic hygiene by washing his hands before touching the bandages and the wound. Although it hurt Zack when Kat cleaned the wound, he knew she was helping him and being as careful as she could, so he had turned away and bitten his lip to keep from crying out. Kat said the penicillin, which she called an antibiotic, would make Zack feel better. He didn't understand why, but he took her word for it.

Kat had also put his arm in a sling and said that should help with the swelling and the pain. Not having his arm hanging down had already made him feel better. He wished that Kat hadn't left him alone in the big house, though. She had put him in Sarah's bedroom, which had its own television and remote control, but he didn't turn the television on. Being in a strange house alone was skeery enough. But having that strange house be in another century was something else. What if something happened and Madison didn't come right back? What would he do? He couldn't even get back to his own time, because he had closed his eyes for most of the trip here. He had no idea which direction to go. Zack knew there was a cave, but apparently only a few people knew where it was.

Thinking about being alone in this future time, with no way to get home to the people he cared about, scared him. Maybe he wasn't ready to move here after all. Looking around the room, he shivered, though the room wasn't cold. The idea of being stuck in this century made him uncomfortable. Staying here because he chose to stay here was different from staying because he wasn't *able* to get home. That thought made him sigh and fight tears that wanted to come to his eyes. Zack was about to stand up, brace himself against the wall, and stumble to the front room to look out the window for Madison, when he heard her come in the front door. Relief swept over him, and he allowed himself to relax back against the pillow.

CHAPTER NINE

MADISON DIDN'T SAY a word when she came through the door. She had noticed that her mother's car was gone, so it meant that Zack was home alone. He might be sleeping, and she didn't want to disturb him. But although she couldn't call out to him and he hadn't called out to her, there was a certain comfort in knowing that someone was in the house waiting for her. It gave her a sense of purpose, a reason for being. Not that she needed that, but it felt good regardless.

"Madison? I'm back here," said Zack.

A feeling of warmth swept over her, and she liked it. It felt good having someone waiting at home for her—and when it was a man who was waiting for her, it was even better. When she lived with the two roommates, one of them was inevitably home when she got home, but the feeling wasn't the same. In that cramped apartment, her main feeling was wanting to be alone.

Zack's voice sounded like it came from Sarah's bedroom. Madison thought that her mother must have put him in that room because it had a television. She headed in that direction. When she walked into the room, she saw him lying in bed propped up with a pillow behind his head. His color seemed better.

She sat down on the side of the bed next to him and said, "Hi. How do you feel?"

"It still hurts, but not as much. I think this helps," he said, indicating the sling.

Madison held up the small sack in her hand. "I got your meds."

"What are meds?" asked Zack.

"Oh, sorry. That's twenty-first-century-speak for medicine. Your next dose is tomorrow morning."

Zack's eyes widened. "*You're* going to give me a shot?"

Madison laughed easily and patted his good arm. "Not to worry, Zack. There shouldn't be any more shots. These are pills."

"Oh, good," Zack said, as he relaxed and looked away embarrassed.

She noticed the book on the bed on the other side of him. "Can I see your book?" she asked.

Zack picked it up and put it on his chest. "Oh, it's just a book I'm reading, that's all."

"I know. Can I see it? Sarah said it was a law book. Did she mean a novel about law?"

"Ah, no. It's just, ah, well, here." Reluctantly, Zack handed her the book.

Madison read the title, *Purdon's Digest of Laws of Pennsylvania.* "Are you from Pennsylvania or something?"

"No, I read all the law books I can get. There aren't many, so I read whatever I can find."

She looked up into his face. "Are you interested in the law?"

Zack looked away and, without looking at her, said, "My dream is to become a lawyer. But before you tell me how crazy that is, I know that it's just a dream." He said it defensively.

"Zack, I don't think it's crazy at all. That's what I'm taking in college. Well, I'm in pre-law now and next year I'll start law school."

Zack's eyes sparkled when he turned to look at her. "*You're* going to be a lawyer? Really? I mean, girls can become lawyers, too?"

Madison tried not to laugh. "It's a different time, Zack. Women can do anything nowadays—at least in the United States and other progressive countries. You have a lot to learn about the twenty-first century!" She thought maybe she shouldn't have said that. Maybe he wasn't interested in learning about this century. Maybe he just wanted to go home and never see this future time again. But she could hope, couldn't she?

Zack leaned toward her. "I'd like to learn, Madison. I'd really like to learn. Will you teach me?"

She smiled at him. "Of course I will, Zack. I'll teach you and show you as much of this world as you're interested in. But for now, you need to rest. You've had a big day. Your body needs time to heal itself." Madison stood up. "Try to rest now. I'll be in later to check on you and make sure you're okay. Rest easy, Zack." She leaned over, kissed him on the forehead, and walked from the room.

It was all she could do as she left the room not to shout for joy. He wanted to be a lawyer! And he wanted to learn about this century. She forced her thoughts to slow down. Just because he wanted to be a lawyer and learn about her century, didn't mean he wanted to *be* a lawyer in *her* century. He was a bright guy. Perhaps he just wanted to accumulate all the knowledge he could about her century, but had no desire to stay. That would be reasonable. It would probably be easier to become a lawyer in his time, anyway.

Madison knew that she had to stop building on the Zack fantasy. Yes, it was a pleasant thought that he was the answer to all her wishes. Because she didn't just want a boyfriend. She wanted a boyfriend who was also a companion and could discuss with her the subject she was most interested in: the law. And hadn't she admitted today that she needed something more in her life? It was almost as if the universe had delivered Zack right to her. Maybe wishes really did come true. All you had to do was think about what you wanted, feel what it would feel like to have it already, and abracadabra, there it was in your life. She laughed at her own joke. It just didn't work that way in the real world.

Although—what if it did? Zack was a man who she was already attracted to, and he wanted to be a lawyer. So they could discuss the law together as she had wanted. And if he *did* decide to stay in her century, he would probably be comfortable staying with her in her house—everything seemed exactly perfect—if only it wasn't a fantasy.

CHAPTER TEN

ZACK WOKE UP in total darkness. Wow! What a crazy dream he'd had! Madison was in it. That wasn't the crazy part, though—he'd had dreams about her before. No, it was about the future! There was an object that you could hold in your hand and talk to people that was called an iPhone. And there was that other thing called a television that had moving pictures on it. Wait until he told Sarah and Matthew about the dream. And he wanted to remember to tell them about the bathroom, too. That was amazing.

Wait. He felt better, and he had felt so bad before. Not that he actually felt good. No, he still didn't feel good. His arm still hurt. But the pain was less, and he didn't feel as uncomfortable. Zack reached out and touched his sore arm. Something was over it. He felt all around. It was a sling! Like in the dream! Maybe Sarah had put it on him while he slept. He pulled the covers off himself and discovered they were different, too. His own blanket had been replaced by a thin blanket with little lumps spaced evenly apart. What was going on?

Zack's eyes had started to adjust to the darkness, and

he looked around. Nothing was clear, it was still too dark for that, but the room didn't look familiar. There was something sitting on the chest of drawers in front of the bed that looked vaguely like the television from the dream. Propping himself up with his good arm, he put his hand out to the bedside table and felt that it had a lamp on it. Feeling around the top of the table, he searched in the darkness for matches. None.

He relaxed back onto the bed. It was starting to dawn on him that it wasn't a fantastic dream after all. It had all been real. Going over everything in his head, he remembered waking up in the morning feeling especially bad, Sarah and Matthew putting him in a wagon, riding through a cave, arriving at Madison's house, and her mother, Kat, who was some kind of nurse, putting a needle in his bum. As he reached back, his bum still felt sore. It's all real, he thought. He was in the future!

His book lay beside him on the bed, and it reminded him of his conversation with Madison. *She* was going to be a lawyer! And she hadn't laughed at him when he said he wanted to become a lawyer. It wasn't like anyone in town had actually laughed at him. Matthew and Josiah would never do that. It was the way they looked at him when he mentioned it—almost like they felt sorry for him for wanting that. He didn't want people to laugh at him, and he didn't want people to feel sorry for him just because he wanted to be a lawyer.

He knew why they reacted like that, though. What were the chances of a poor boy like him going to law school? It was expensive, and he had no money. He didn't even have the money to get there, or money for books, or any of the many requirements that would be necessary for him to attend law school. Although he could probably find a lawyer in some town close by who might take him on as an apprentice—that wasn't the same. It wasn't a real education. Zack loved to read, and he loved to read about the law. Besides, since Josiah had told him that he had gone to school to become a lawyer, that's exactly what Zack wanted to do. It didn't matter that Josiah had given it all up to move out west and become the sheriff of Red Bluff. It only mattered that he had done it, and Zack wanted to do that, too.

Then his thoughts drifted to where he was. In the *future*. A future where even *girls* could go to law school. If girls could, then surely he could find a way. Could he stay in the future and leave behind everything and everyone that he cared about? If it meant becoming a lawyer, he could.

And the thought of maybe sharing that future with Madison made it an even better idea. Now that he knew the truth about Sarah, Jenna, and Granny—that they had moved to the past to be with the men they loved—it made his thoughts of maybe moving to the future for the same reason seem almost possible, almost realistic.

Then he remembered a quote that he had read from Ralph Waldo Emerson, one of his favorite authors: "Dare to live the life you have dreamed for yourself. Go forward and make your dreams come true." He had always considered his wish to be a lawyer just a dream. Now he had the chance to make that dream come true. But how would Madison feel about him moving to her century? Yes, she had said she would teach him about it. But teaching someone and sharing a life with that person were two different matters. He would absorb everything she had to say about life in this century and everything about becoming a lawyer before he even mentioned to her that he was considering moving here.

Was he considering moving here? Was he *truly* considering that? No, he wasn't considering. He had decided. This time, this twenty-first century—more than one hundred years in his future—would be his new home. He would make it work. And he would become a lawyer, just like he always wanted.

But another thought crept into his mind. Madison. With her long dark hair, and eyes so dark you could barely see the pupil—he loved looking at her, looking into her eyes. Although he had only spoken to her a couple of times before, he had always liked her. Now, being around her in her home, in her own environment, he liked her even more. Yes, he wanted to be a lawyer, but he also really wanted to be with Madison.

CHAPTER ELEVEN

MADISON THOUGHT SHE heard Zack stirring, but the light hadn't gone on, so she stayed in her room. She didn't want to disturb him if he was still sleeping. He didn't need any medication tonight, so she didn't have to worry about that.

Smiling to herself, she realized how much she liked having another person in the house. Not that she had ever been afraid living alone in the big house, but it was comforting having someone else there. Someone else who she could potentially really fall for. She had to be careful, though, falling for someone from another century without knowing what he thought. She didn't need heartache to disturb her life right now. But love—yes, she had time for love. Plenty of time for love—with the right person, of course. Was Zack the right person? Although she didn't know, it was looking more and more like he was.

After she had left Zack's room, she had spent most of the rest of the day studying for the LSAT—Law School Admission Test. Although she had signed up for an LSAT prep class for her first quarter in the fall, she wanted to make double sure that she was prepared. She had bought several books, had downloaded a sample test from the internet, and had been working with that. So far though, what she had seen were just basic reasoning questions that she had seen on those online IQ—intelligence quotient—tests.

If Pookie is a black bear who likes strawberries, and his wife, Puff, is a brown bear who likes blueberries, what color will their children be? Well, not exactly that bad, but the questions felt like that.

Madison heard Zack cough. She thought that he must be up, so she walked down the hall toward his bedroom, stood outside, and said softly, "Zack?"

"Yes, I'm awake, now, Madison."

She walked into the bedroom. "Did you sleep well?"

"Yeah, I didn't realize how much I needed more sleep. I'm feeling a little better now. Where are the matches for this light? I couldn't find them."

"Zack, it's the twenty-first century! No more matches! Here, let me show you. Put your hand here on the base of the lamp. Feel that little knob? Turn that."

Zack followed her instructions, and the light came on. "It's going to take awhile for me to figure out all these neat things in your time, Madison. But right now, I have to use the necessary—I mean the bathroom. I think I can make it on my own, though." He stood up shakily, and Madison helped him out the door and waited till he could brace himself on the wall to go into the bathroom.

She walked to the living room, bent over in front of the bookcase, and pulled a book from the shelf. Then she went back to Zack's room to wait for him. After hearing the toilet flush several times, she called out, "Zack, what are you doing in there?"

"Oh, this is so neat. I like to watch the water swirl down!"

"You need to stop, dude. Wash your hands and come back in here."

When Zack returned and lay back on the bed, Madison spoke, "You have to learn something about the twenty-first century, Zack. It's polluted."

"I know what polluted means, but I don't understand what you mean about this century being polluted."

"Because of cars and factories, we have put junk into the air. So the air we now breathe is not clean. Red Bluff's air is still pretty good, though. If you went to Los Angeles or another big city, the air is so bad that you can see a brown haze. It's disgusting. And because of the factories, we have polluted our water. So the clean water needs protecting. What I'm trying to say is that you can't waste water like that!"

"Oh! Sorry, I didn't know."

"I know. That's why I told you. You have a lot of catching up to do on the twenty-first century. Let's see, I told you about the lamp, you already know about the remote control for the television," she pointed to the remote on the bedside table, "and tomorrow I'll show you the kitchen and the rest of the house. There are some things that you are not going to believe! And I still have to give you a ride in the car!"

"What's a car?"

"It's like a stagecoach, but it goes without horses. You'll love it. That's tomorrow. Tonight, I brought you this." She handed him the book that she had retrieved from the living room.

He looked at the book she handed him and held it to his chest. "*A Time to Kill.* Is it some kind of law book?"

"It's a novel, but it's about lawyers. I think you'll like it. And the author, John Grisham, has a bunch of other books about lawyers. I'll show you where they're kept tomorrow. You can even take them back with you and return them later. You can come here any time to get more books. It will be like a library for you! Do you have a horse?"

Zack looked down, and Madison knew it was a bad question. "I used to. Echo is a black and white pinto horse, very gentle, great personality." Zack hesitated, and Madison didn't say anything, waiting for him to go on. "After my dad died and I had so little money, I couldn't afford to keep him anymore, so I sold him to Ezra at the livery stable. At first, I'd go visit him every day. Then I thought that it would be better for Echo and me not to see each other anymore. It was painful." Another hesitation, but Madison could tell that he wasn't finished talking. "I still see him around now and then, and although I know that Ezra at the livery stable treats him well, I can only hope the people who hire him out do the same. I know people have offered to buy him from Ezra—Echo is very pretty—Ezra hasn't sold him, as a favor to me, I guess, although I haven't visited him for years." Zack sighed.

"Why is he named Echo?"

Zack brightened. "Because when you talk to him, he 'talks' back. It's really neat. He'll nicker right back at you like he's answering. I loved that about him."

"Have you seen him lately?"

"A couple of weeks ago was the last time when I saw someone riding him back into the livery."

Madison thought for a minute. "How much does it cost to buy a horse in the nineteenth century?"

"I sold him to Ezra for seven dollars, why?"

"Do you have any money in your pocket?"

Zack shook his head. "I know what you're thinking, Madison, and even if I could afford to buy him back, I couldn't afford to board him at the livery. I have nowhere to keep him."

Madison put out her hand to Zack. "Do you have any money? Let me see it."

Zack reached into his pocket and pulled out one silver dollar, two half dollars, a quarter, and a penny. Madison turned over each coin inspecting it carefully.

"Why are you looking at my coins like that?"

"Times have changed, Zack. Some old coins are worth a lot of money. Money is made differently now, and old money—money from your time—is worth a lot more than face value. You could still spend any of this money here, but you can get more for it if you take it to a coin dealer. I know Aunt Jenna cashed in some gold coins for fifteen hundred dollars each!"

That got Zack interested. "Really? Do you think these are worth anything?"

"I don't know. They're all silver, and I don't think silver is worth as much. But we can check."

"How? When? Can we do it now?"

"Calm down, Zack. You need to get more sleep so you can heal."

"Oh, come on, Madison! I want to know!"

"Zack, you need to get some sleep." She put the coins on the bedside table and asked, "Do you need anything else?"

"Yeah. Why does this blanket have lumps in it?"

"Oh!" Madison laughed. "It's an electric blanket. If you get cold during the night, then flick this switch right here," she showed him the blanket control that sat on the bedside table, "and it will warm you right up. It has different heat levels, also, so you can turn it up or down to make yourself comfortable."

"Wow," said Zack. "Good night, Madison. Thank you for all your help."

"Good night, Zack. Sleep well, and I'll see you in the morning." Madison turned off the light, closed the door most of the way, and walked to her own room down the hall.

CHAPTER TWELVE

ZACK DIDN'T KNOW how he could possibly sleep. His first impulse normally would have been to turn the light back on and read the new book that Madison had just given him. That was before she had told him about the money. He reached out and felt the coins on the table. Could these coins really bring him enough money to buy back Echo and pay for his board without worry? Zack hoped so. That horse meant a lot to him, both personally, and as a connection to his dead parents. Getting Echo back was right up there with becoming a lawyer and being with the girl of his dreams—Madison. Could he possibly have it all? He hoped so.

Thinking about Echo, the new book, and all the experiences of the day tuckered him out. That, and the weakness he still felt from the wound in his arm, helped put him to sleep. He slept peacefully through the night and woke up refreshed. His arm didn't hurt as much, it wasn't as swollen, and he wasn't disoriented at all—he knew exactly where he was—the twenty-first century—with Madison.

Picking up his head and using his good arm, he

propped the pillow up behind him, so he could look around the room. The television sat on the chest of drawers directly in front of him. A heavy curtain over the window prevented much light from getting into the room, but he could still see clearly. There was a door on the side wall, but it didn't have a handle, only a little metal-lined hole. Besides the lamp on the bedside table, there was a light on the ceiling above his head. He wondered where the knob was for that. If it was on the side of it, then people in the twenty-first century would have to be very tall! There was no wood stove in the room—but Zack didn't remember seeing a wood stove in the living room, either. Since they had lights that didn't need matches, and the amazing bathroom, then there was probably some heat source that didn't require a wood stove.

Zack liked it here. He already knew that he didn't want to leave. Ever. He wanted to stay here with Madison, go to school to become a lawyer, and live happily ever after. Of course, Madison would have something to say about that. Allowing his mind to wander, he speculated whether they still had marriage in the twenty-first century. Yes, they did. Jenna had married Josiah, Sarah had married Matthew, and even Granny had married Edward. It wouldn't have happened that easily if marriage was foreign to them. That suited Zack. The idea of marriage suited him.

But before any of that could happen, he needed to get back to the nineteenth century, buy back Echo, and say good-bye to everyone in town. Especially Matthew and Sarah. Since Matthew had married Sarah, she helped around the saloon as much as Zack did. So he didn't need to feel bad about leaving. Besides, they didn't need an extra man around since they were new-married and all. No, his moving to the future would be good for everyone. He only hoped that Madison would agree.

The clock on the chest of drawers must be another of the twenty-first-century inventions. It didn't have a face on it, only numbers. It said 6:30, so it must mean half past six. Zack wondered what time Madison would wake up. He didn't want to disturb her. Then he saw the book on the bedside table. Oh, good! He could read until she woke up. When Zack looked up again to check the clock, an hour had passed. A noise coming from the other room sounded like a toilet flushing—but not the one by his bedroom. Would there be two bathrooms in one house? Why would anyone need more than one bathroom in a house? It didn't make sense to him. But he was from a time more than a hundred years ago. What did he know?

After putting the book down, Zack stretched and sat up in bed. No dizziness. He almost felt good. Standing up slowly, just in case, he walked slowly toward the bathroom without having to hold on to the wall. Although he did have his arm extended if he needed to catch himself. While he was in the bathroom, he inspected the bathtub. A movable glass door enclosed the tub, and there was a faucet high up on the wall. Why would there be two faucets for one bathtub? And the lower faucet had three handles. Hot, cold, and what? What would the third handle be for? More twenty-first-century puzzles. He'd have to ask Madison.

Returning to his room, he put his clothes on. He would have liked to change them, but no one—including him—thought to bring his other set of clothes. These weren't that dirty, though. He'd only worn them for a week. Although he had slept in them the night he didn't feel good. But they'd be fine for now.

Picking up the remote control from the bedside table, Zack sat on the end of the bed and switched on the television. Moving pictures came on, but they weren't real people—they were paintings or something. Clicking the remote control past several more channels, he came to one where they talked about the weather. They showed a map of the United States and talked about what weather was expected in each area. It amazed him. The future, and all the fascinating inventions in it, captivated him. It made him even more certain that he wanted to stay here. He clicked more times until he came back to the moving paintings. The people and animals did and said funny things, and it made him laugh.

"Cartoons? You're watching cartoons?" asked Madison from his doorway.

"Is that what they're called? They're funny!"

"Oh, you're already dressed. I thought you might want to shower first."

"What's 'shower'?"

"Come here, let me show you," said Madison.

Zack followed her into the bathroom. She stopped in front of the bathtub with the glass doors. Reaching in, she turned the handles by the bottom faucet and water came out the top faucet.

"Oh!" said Zack, surprised. "Why does it do that?"

"That's what a shower is. You stand under the water, so you don't have to fill the tub up. You wash and rinse as you're standing there. Want to try it?"

"Maybe later. I want to find out if my coins are worth any money first. Now that there's a chance to get Echo back, I can't think of anything else." Except you, Madison, but Zack didn't say that.

"Okay, we can do that, but I think you should eat first. Aren't you hungry? You didn't eat anything at all yesterday, did you?"

"I didn't feel good enough to eat, yesterday. But yes, I am hungry now."

"You have to take a pill this morning, too. Mom would be upset if I forget to give it to you." Madison walked back into Zack's bedroom and retrieved the bottle of pills. "Come on, let's go into the kitchen. More wonders await!"

CHAPTER THIRTEEN

AS MADISON LED the way into the kitchen, she wondered if all the marvels of the twenty-first century would be enough to hold Zack here. Or would *she* be enough to hold Zack here? The more time she spent with him, the more she liked him. There was something about him that felt almost *familiar* to her. Although she didn't know him very well, it was almost like he already belonged here, belonged with her.

"And this is the kitchen. Wait until you see the cool things in here!" said Madison, as she motioned with her hand and opened the door. "This is the refrigerator. Put your hand inside."

"It's cold! How does it do that? Where's the ice?"

"Up here." Madison opened the freezer above the main part of the refrigerator and pulled out a single ice cube tray.

"That little bit of ice keeps this big thing cold?"

"No. Up here is where you keep food that needs to be frozen."

"What makes it cold, though?"

"I don't know the workings of a refrigerator, Zack.

You'll have to look it up online."

"Look it up where?"

"Online. Oh! Wait till you learn about the internet! But first, the rest of the kitchen." Madison walked over to the sink and the dishwasher beside it. "You've already seen running water in the bathroom, but look at this." She opened the door to the dishwasher. "This is the dishwasher. You put your dirty dishes in here, add soap, close the door, start it up, and voila! Clean dishes!"

"Do it now! Let me see!"

"Well, it's not exactly 'voila' . . . it takes an hour. But still, amazing, don't you think?"

Zack nodded. "No more washing glasses! Wouldn't Matthew love something like that!"

Madison walked over to the electric flat top stove. "This is the stove. You turn on these dials here, and the top of it gets hot. You can boil water on top here, or whatever. Inside," she opened the oven door, "is where you cook food. And step over here." She retrieved a cup from the cabinet, filled it with water, put it into the microwave, and turned it on. "This really is 'voila.' The water will be hot in a minute." The bell rang, and Madison removed the cup. "Feel it."

Zack stuck his finger in and pulled it out quickly. "It's hot! This is all cool, Madison. Now show me the internet!"

"Well, don't we look better today," said Kat from the doorway. "You must be feeling good today, young patient of mine."

"Much better, Kat. Thank you," said Zack.

Kat walked over to Zack and put her hand to his forehead. "You still have a fever, but not as bad as yesterday. Come. Sit at the table and let me examine your arm and take your temperature." Zack sat down at the table. "I hope you took your first pill this morning, Zack."

"Oh, sorry, Mom. I brought the pills in here to give him one, but we got sidetracked with the appliances. Here's the bottle. I'll get him a glass of water."

Kat reached into her medical kit and retrieved the thermometer. Then she ran it across his forehead. "Very good. It's gone down to one hundred degrees. You still don't feel very good, do you?"

"No, Ma'am."

"But I bet with these twenty-first-century wonders all around you, you're too excited to notice. Here, take the pill with the water Madison brought you." Kat opened the pill bottle and shook out one pill into the cap, then dropped it into Zack's open hand. After he swallowed the pill, Kat said, "Now let me look at your arm." Zack put his arm on the table, so she could see it. "Yes, much better. It's healing nicely. Less red. Not as hot. Not as swollen. It's all good, Zack. You're healing well."

"Is it all right if I take him to the coin dealer today?" asked Madison.

"Definitely no. He needs to rest. It would even be good if you could leave him alone for some time today, so he can rest." Turning to Zack, she said, "Zack, you need to take care of this. I know you're healing quickly, but you don't want it to get infected again. You need to take the pills twice a day and take it easy. No running around."

"When can I take him out, Mom?"

"I'll stop by tomorrow to check on him. But let's see how he is Monday. You'll be at your new job, right? I'll stop by before I go to work and check on him. I'll leave a note whether he can go out or not."

"You can just tell Zack. You don't need to leave a note," said Madison.

Kat smiled and looked at Zack. "It's not that I don't trust you, Zack. It's that I don't want any misinterpretations of what I say." Then, turning to Madison, she said, "If Zack needs anything in town, Madison, you can get it for him."

"I thought it would be more fun for Zack if he could go to the coin dealer himself."

"That's fine. He can. But not yet. I have to run now. Bye, sweetie." Kat leaned over and kissed Madison on the forehead. "Love you."

"Love you, too, Mom," said Madison.

Turning to Zack, Kat said, "Bye, Zack. I'll stop by tomorrow to see how you're doing. Take your pills and TAKE IT EASY!"

CHAPTER FOURTEEN

"YOUR MOM IS so nice," said Zack. "It's so nice of her to do all this for me and check on me every day and everything."

"Yeah, for a mom, she's pretty cool," said Madison. "Okay, now that Mom's come to visit, and you've seen all the miraculous devices in the twenty-first century, how 'bout we eat? I'm starved!"

"I'm a little hungry, too."

"I'm not much of a cook. Are eggs and toast okay?"

"I'm a cook! I can cook something for us!" said Zack, standing up.

"Not today, Zack. You're still recovering. Wait till you're well, and I'll let you cook all you want."

"Okay," and he sat back in the chair. "Eggs and toast sound fine."

Madison fried some eggs and put two slices of bread in the toaster. She put the eggs in front of Zack and sat at the table next to him. "The toast will be up in a minute."

"Where did you put the bread?"

"Oh, I never thought to show you the toaster! You put

bread into it, and it comes out crispy."

"Why don't you use the microwave?"

"Microwaves heat food, but they don't get it crispy. Toasters work perfect for that. Oh! There it goes!"

Madison retrieved the toast and brought it over to the table. Zack took a piece, dabbed it in his eggs, and put it in his mouth.

"You're a better cook than you think. This is delicious, Madison."

"Thanks, Zack. It's only eggs. I'm not completely helpless."

"What are we going to do today?" asked Zack.

"*You* are going to rest today. But since we can't go to the coin dealer, we can at least look up the coins online and see what they're worth."

"How do we do that?"

"Wait until you see the computer, Zack. I think you'll love it. It's better than anything else you've seen so far!"

After they finished breakfast and Madison had put the dishes into the dishwasher, she said, "Zack, you get your coins, and I'll get my computer."

Zack walked back into his bedroom and picked up the coins from the bedside table. He wondered what kind of miraculous object a computer could be. Between the flushing toilet, the television, the dishwasher, the microwave, and the iPhone, it was hard to believe there was something even better. Returning to the living room, he saw Madison sitting on the couch looking at something in front of her. It didn't seem all that miraculous as he walked up and sat beside her.

"This is a laptop computer, Zack. I'll start you from the beginning, because you can use it when I'm at work."

"It's like a small television, except the pictures aren't

moving," said Zack.

"Oh, there's plenty of moving pictures, if you know where to find them. But first, Google. If you want to find information about any subject you could possibly think of, type it in here. Have you used a typewriter? The keys are still the same, even from your time."

"What's a typewriter?"

"Really? You don't know what a typewriter is? I thought they were invented already. Let's look it up online."

Zack watched as Madison typed in "when were typewriters invented" onto the Google page. "Don't you need a question mark?" he asked.

"With Google, it doesn't matter. Here. See all the different possibilities that come up? These links will all say something about when typewriters were invented. Let's click on this first one from Wikipedia. That's like an online encyclopedia. Ah, yes, here it is. Look at the second paragraph. See what it says?"

Zack read aloud from the screen, "After their invention in the 1860s—"

Madison interrupted him. "That's why you don't know what a typewriter is! It was barely invented in 1870! Well, anyway, you'll have to learn the keyboard. What else would you like to look up?"

"Like what?"

"Anything you could think of that you want to know."

"Let's look up the coins! I really want to know about that. Since you told me the coins might help me buy Echo back, I can't think of anything else." That was mostly true, because Zack wasn't going to tell Madison that he couldn't keep his mind off *her*.

"Okay, the coins," said Madison. Zack watched as

Madison typed "coin values from the 1800s" into the Google page. "Here we are. Let's start with the dollars. They're probably worth more. What date is your dollar?"

Zack looked at the silver dollar in his hand. "1859," he told her.

"Is there a letter by it? S, D, or something like that? I don't know much about coins, but I know most of them have a letter that represents where they were minted."

"S," said Zack. "1859 S."

"Here it is. Depending on what condition it's in, it's worth three hundred dollars, at least. There are several different categories of their condition, but I don't know enough about them to tell you what they mean. You can look it up later, if you want."

"Three hundred dollars? Really? I could buy Echo back and board him for more than a year with that!" As Zack said that, he thought that he didn't want to board Echo in the 1800s, he wanted him here. In the future. With him. With Madison. But he kept silent.

"Now let's look up your other coins," said Madison. "What dates are your half dollars?"

"1855 S and 1856 S."

"The 1855 is worth at least five hundred! You're worth a fortune, Zack!"

"Wow! It might be worth more than the dollar! That doesn't make sense to me, but not much of the twenty-first century does. What about the other one?"

"Oh, it's not worth as much, unfortunately. Maybe a hundred dollars."

"That's still a lot of money. What about the quarter? It's an 1869 S."

"It's worth maybe four hundred dollars. More than the half dollar!"

"And the penny is an 1867, with no letter."

"One hundred. Remember that it all depends on the condition of the coin. If it's in bad condition, the price will be less, but if it's in *really* good condition, the price could go up considerably. Since your coins are only ten or fifteen years old, they could be worth more. I think you're rich!"

Zack held the coins to his heart and smiled at Madison. He thought about how wonderful it would be to get Echo back and even more wonderful to live here in this century with Madison. But did she feel the same way? He didn't know enough about women to know, but he hoped she did.

Music started playing, and Madison reached for her iPhone. "Hello!" Then she turned to Zack and said, "Zack, I'll be right back. Go ahead. Try it. You can look up anything." Pointing to the keyboard, she added, "Click here to get back to Google. Press here to click. Be back in a few." Madison walked out of the room as she talked on the phone.

At first, Zack felt afraid to touch the laptop computer. It seemed so powerful that he wondered what would happen if he did something wrong. Then he decided that if he was determined to live in the twenty-first century, he had to learn to operate the different objects here. Starting with a laptop computer. Starting now.

He moved over in front of the computer, pressed the button, and clicked where Madison had showed him. The Google page came up. What should he look up? What did he want to know? Everything! He wanted to know everything about this wonderful century that he was now a part of. At least he hoped he was a part of it —that is, more than just staying long enough for his arm to heal. What did he want? Besides Madison, that is. To become a lawyer. Zack typed in "how do you become a lawyer." It was hard picking out the letters on the keyboard since they weren't in alphabetical order, and he could only use one hand. But he managed and clicked the search button.

The page changed, and Zack smiled at his success. He chose the second option: 5 Ways to Become a Lawyer in the United States. It talked about high school. Zack wondered what high school was. Did it mean college—a higher school than regular school? No, he didn't think so. Madison had mentioned college. So what was high school? He moved his fingers trying to see farther down the page. Finally, the page moved, although Zack wasn't sure what he had done to make it move. Attend a four-year college. What? A four-year college and *then* law school? Wow. That was a commitment. Did he really want to do that? He smiled to himself. Yes. Yes he did.

Zack thought he heard Madison coming. Since he didn't want her to know yet what he was thinking, he clicked back to the Google page and moved over so she could sit in front of the computer when she returned.

CHAPTER FIFTEEN

WHEN MADISON WALKED into the living room and saw Zack, she abruptly stopped. As he sat there, not yet aware of her presence, he gazed at the computer screen with an innocence that you might see on the face of a child. And he was beautiful. His hair, a little unkempt but still attractive, was jet black. Although she couldn't see his eyes from there, she knew they were large and dark brown. His long lashes would have been better suited for a woman, but they looked wonderful on him—they added to his innocence. Was she falling in love with him? She hardly knew him, how could that be possible? And yet, she thought that was exactly what was happening.

Zack turned to look at her and smiled. "Hi, Madison!"

Madison returned his smile and said, "Oh, just girl-talk. It was one of my old roommates." She sat down beside him. "Did you just sit there the whole time waiting for me? I wanted you to poke around some."

"Oh, I did. It took awhile to get the page to move down, but I somehow made it happen. I'm still not sure how, though!"

"Just do this." She showed him how to move his fingers on the trackpad. "See? Oh, I need to plug it in now."

"Plug it in? What do you mean?"

"I'll have to explain to you about electricity, Zack. I don't think your time gets it for a few more years. Come with me," said Madison, as she stood up and walked toward her bedroom. Once inside, she put the laptop on her desk and showed Zack how to plug it in. "Let's go out to see the horses now."

As they walked toward the barn, Zack noticed the cars parked on the other side of the house. "What are *those*?"

"Those are cars—like a stagecoach without horses, kind of. When Mom gives the okay for you to go out, I'll take you for a ride! We'll take the car when we go see the coin dealer."

When they reached the barn, Madison relaxed. Often, like now, she didn't even realize she was tense, but walking into the barn, with its horsey smells, always immediately relaxed her. Madison stroked Paisley's face as she walked by. "This is Mom's mare, Paisley. And this is my boy, Chaco. Isn't he handsome?"

"He's beautiful," said Zack, stroking the horse's face with his good arm. Chaco nickered at Zack and nuzzled him.

"He likes you! Maybe when your arm is better we can go riding. Mom doesn't ride very often, and Paisley could use some exercise."

Looking around, Zack said, "This is a nice barn."

"Aunt Jenna had it specially built. See the doors on the other side of the horses' stalls? They open out onto a paddock, and the horses can open the doors themselves."

"Why would they need to open the doors themselves?"

"Jenna's parents, my grandparents, died in a fire in the

old barn trying to get the horses out. So Jenna had this specially made."

"Oh, wow. That's a sad story. I'm sorry."

"It's been a few years now. I try not to think about it. But sometimes when I'm in here alone, I feel like my grandparents are talking to me. I like it." Zack nodded his head but didn't say anything. Madison didn't know if he believed her or not. She hoped that he did. It was early enough in the relationship that she wanted to continue thinking of him as perfect. Relationship! What was she thinking? She didn't even know if he liked her or not. Besides, he lived in another century! She told herself, get real, girl.

Zack interrupted her thoughts. "And they get hay automatically from that?"

"Yes, exactly. Most days, unless I close the gate, they can go out to the pasture themselves and eat all the grass they want. But they also have constant access to the hay. At first they gained weight, but after they got used to having it there all the time, they didn't eat as much. Come on, I'll show you the pasture."

Madison opened the gate to Chaco's stall and held it open for Zack to walk in. She noticed how he kept his hand on Chaco as he walked past him. He knew horses. She liked that. They walked out into the paddock, and Chaco followed them. Madison climbed onto the back fence that faced the pasture. She noticed that Zack climbed up with only his good arm, but didn't complain about it. He wasn't a complainer—she liked that, too.

"You have cows!"

"Yeah, they're Aunt Jenna's. I'm just taking care of them until she sells them. It won't be much longer, I don't think."

"Where are their horns?"

"They're called *polled* cattle. That means they don't have horns. Most ranchers don't have cattle with horns anymore because they're more trouble."

"So much has changed," said Zack, as he climbed back down from the fence.

"Let's go back in now," said Madison. As she walked by Chaco, she stopped and gave him a big hug. She walked toward the barn, but saw that Zack had stopped and given Chaco a hug, too. That made Madison smile.

CHAPTER SIXTEEN

As THEY WALKED back to the house, Zack asked, "What's high school?"

"They didn't have high school in the 1800s?"

"They might have, but not where I was. What is it? Do they mean college?"

"No. That's right, you probably went to the one-room schoolhouse, didn't you?"

"Yes, I did—when I was in school. Much of my childhood, I didn't go to school. But my father thought education was important, so he brought me books whenever he could."

"High school is the last school you go to *before* college—although some people never go to college, even now. Anyway, first you go to grammar school, then middle school or junior high, and last is high school. It's grades nine through twelve or ten through twelve—depending on where you live. But you need a high school diploma to get into college nowadays."

"Oh," said Zack, disappointed.

"Although for those who never finished high school, there's always the GED. That stands for General Equivalency Diploma. Then you would also need to take the SAT, Scholastic Aptitude Test, or the ACT test, American College Testing—probably both if you only have a GED. Why?"

"Ah, just wondering," said Zack. "I ran across the term 'high school' when I was on your computer."

When they stepped into the house, Madison walked toward the couch in the living room. "While we wait for the computer to recharge, let me show you some music videos. I think you'll like them."

"Sure," said Zack. Any time spent with Madison was time he enjoyed.

The afternoon and evening flew by, and before Zack realized, it was already time to go to sleep. "Zack, if you want to watch TV tonight, just close your door and keep the sound low. I can't hear it from my room."

"TV? Is that television?"

"Yeah. It's the abbreviation that everybody uses when they talk about televisions."

"Okay, thanks. I'll probably just read instead. Good night, Madison." He watched as she walked down the hall away from him, and he sighed. Although he didn't know when he would return to the past, he knew it would be too soon.

As he lay in bed and thought about the new wonders he had seen, like electricity, the internet, toasters, and cows without horns, it amazed him how easily he accepted it all. It was completely foreign to how he had lived the first twenty-two years of his life, and yet he took to it like a horse to grass. He thought about when electricity might reach the nineteenth century and realized he could look that up on the internet. But it didn't matter. What happened in the nineteenth century had no bearing on the Zack Murphy of today. Zack was starting to consider himself more and more as a man of the twenty-first century. He liked it here, and he didn't want to leave.

Then his thoughts drifted to the horses, Chaco and Paisley. It had been so long since he had touched a horse. Although he had ridden one when he and the other men rescued Sarah and again when they went after the men who had kidnapped her, Echo hadn't been available either time. Ezra, at the livery, had apologized, but Zack was secretly glad. It would have been awful to ride Echo and then have to leave him there, not knowing when he could ride him again. So when he did ride out those two times on the rented horse, he just got on and rode. There was more on his mind those two days with no time to stroke the horse or think about how wonderful a horse smells. Not everyone understood that. But Zack had seen Madison hug Chaco. He knew that she would understand. And that made him like her even more.

CHAPTER SEVENTEEN

MADISON COULDN'T BELIEVE how fast Sunday flew by. It started when her mother arrived in the morning to check on Zack. His infection was significantly improved, and he had no fever. She said that he could take a short walk, and Monday he could go to the coin dealer. After she left, Zack was so excited about riding in a car—to the coin dealer—that he could hardly contain himself. Madison had encouraged his excitement and said, "Go ahead! Celebrate!" Zack jumped up and down and waved his good arm in the air, making Madison laugh.

She enjoyed him. She enjoyed every minute with him. On their walk, after Madison pointed out the neighborhood, they talked and talked. It felt amazing that they had so much in common although more than a hundred years separated them. Madison liked everything about him: his looks, his intelligence, and the way his eyes got big when she showed him something new and miraculous from the twenty-first century. First he'd look at her like he didn't believe it. Then he'd get this huge smile on his face as he realized how cool it was. There was only one thing she didn't like about him—he wasn't from her time.

Of course, none of it even mattered if he didn't feel the same about her. And she had no idea. Judging by the way he sometimes looked at her, she was sure he felt the same way. Other times, he acted almost aloof, or as if he was deliberately trying to keep her away. It confused her. She didn't know if she should say anything about her feelings or not—she didn't want to scare him away. Except that she didn't want him to *get* away either. Maybe he felt the same way but didn't have the nerve to say anything. How much exposure could he have had to women in that small town? Madison didn't even think there were any women his age in the old Red Bluff. Should she say something? Or maybe put her hand on his leg? Or maybe she should really go for it and kiss him! Then she'd know!

The phone rang and interrupted her thoughts. "Law Office. Yes. I'll connect you." Madison put the phone down and continued with her typing. She didn't mind the job. Her Aunt Jenna had gotten her the job at the law office where she used to be a lawyer. Madison had worked there every summer since her first year in college. She was such a good worker that they had asked her back for a second summer, and again for the third summer. Since she wasn't technically a law student yet, almost all she did was typing and filing. Although last year she had done some go-fer work to the courthouse. That was fun.

She sighed. What was she going to do about Zack? Should she make the first move or wait for him? Madison knew she needed to talk to someone about it—someone more experienced than her friends. Her mother might be a good choice in a different situation. Since she had given birth to Madison while she was still a teenager, they were very close in age—only sixteen years apart. But Madison didn't know how her mother felt about Zack or about his being from the past. She had asked her advice before about some nameless man. But it was something altogether different asking her advice on someone that her mother actually knew. No, her mother was not a possibility. Maybe Granny. She may be old, but she was as sharp as they come.

That idea brought new thoughts to Madison, thoughts that had wanted to be acknowledged, but Madison hadn't brought them into her consciousness yet. She needed to go back to the past. Although she had intended on riding back with Zack, she could do it in one day. There and back wasn't a long trip at all—she had done that before. No, this time she'd stay overnight. Then she'd have a chance to talk it over with Granny. She lived in the past with a man from the past. If anyone would have good advice, it would be her. Madison smiled to herself and saved the file she was working on.

CHAPTER EIGHTEEN

ZACK DIDN'T KNOW where Sunday went, but he was glad it was Monday. When he was with Madison, a whole day could seem like a minute. He couldn't get enough of her. This morning, he had gotten up at seven so he could have breakfast with her before she left for work. She had sensed his uneasiness and guessed that he was nervous about staying alone. It wasn't exactly correct, but close enough. He was uneasy because he had been wanting to look up subjects on the internet, and he didn't want Madison to know. Namely, getting a GED, taking the SAT and ACT test, and enrolling in college. Zack knew he could do it. He was smart, and he was determined.

Madison had barely pulled out from the driveway when Zack was already sitting in front of the computer. First he typed in "how to study for the GED test." By clicking from one page to the next, he discovered a lot of information—much of which disappointed him. Although he knew he could do it, when he realized the test contained questions about science, math, history, geography, and more, it overwhelmed him. Most of what was on the test were events and discoveries that hadn't yet happened in his century. Studying for the test would feel like starting school from the beginning. He knew how to read, but the information he read would all be new to him. Zack set his jaw and decided that reading was enough. He could do it, and he *would* do it.

After clicking around more pages, he wrote down names of books that would help him learn the information. All he had to do was find a bookstore. There were no bookstores in the old Red Bluff except the occasional book that showed up at the Ralston General Store. But in the *new* Red Bluff, surely there were bookstores. Finding one was another matter.

Wait. Madison had said that you could find anything on the internet. Going back to the Google search page, Zack typed in "bookstores in Red Bluff." Reading through the listing, he realized there was more than one Red Bluff. He'd have to narrow it down. Back at the Google search page, he changed the search to "bookstores in Red Bluff, Colorado." Three bookstores came up, but he had no idea where the addresses were. In *his* Red Bluff, there was only Main Street, Back Street, and East Street.

Zack frowned, sighed, and decided to look up more information about coins. Everything hinged on making money with the coins. He knew the coins in his pocket would make him enough money to buy back and keep Echo. Although Zack had worked for Matthew the past few years for barely more than his room and board, he still considered himself an enterprising young fellow. And he had an idea; and he thought it was a good one.

Zack spent the rest of the day researching coins and taking careful notes—only some of which would serve him when he sold the initial coins to the coin dealer.

When Madison pulled up in front of the house at exactly five fifteen as she had told him, Zack was ready.

As he stepped into the car, Madison handed him the seat belt and showed him how to buckle it. "This is so cool, Madison! The seats are really comfortable—not like a stagecoach at all!"

"A car isn't much like a stagecoach at all, but it was the best comparison I could think of!"

As they pulled away, Zack asked, "Can you go faster?"

Madison laughed. "Just like a man! Wanting to drive faster and faster! If we have time after the coin dealer, I'll take you on the highway so you can see how fast we can go."

Zack nodded his head. "All right. How was work today?"

Madison didn't say anything for a minute. But when she stopped the car at a sign that said "STOP," she turned and looked at him with a wistful expression on her face. "Work was fine today, Zack. Thank you for asking. I appreciate that."

"Did you enjoy it?"

"Yes, it wasn't bad. It will be better when I get to do actual law work instead of just typing and filing, but it is a good start for me. How was your day?"

"I spent most of the day on the internet." He patted his shirt pocket. "I have lots of information here to help me at the coin shop."

Madison glanced at him, smiled, and kept driving. "You are the resourceful one, aren't you?"

Zack smiled and pushed forward against the seat belt like he wanted the car to go faster. A few minutes later, Madison parked the car in front of the coin dealer. They stepped out of the car, and Madison put a couple of coins into the parking meter.

“What’s that? Why are you putting money in there?”

“It’s a parking meter. We have to pay for parking. But we won’t be long. It’s not much.” She turned and headed toward the door. “Come on. Let’s go in.”

CHAPTER NINETEEN

ZACK AND MADISON walked into the store and up to the counter. Reaching into his pocket, Zack plunked the coins down on the counter. "Would you be interested in buying these?"

The coin dealer looked at all of them before he picked the dollar up. "They all look in really good condition. Yes, I'm interested. Let's see," he turned the dollar over in his hands, "I'll give you five hundred for this one."

"Did you see the condition of the back?" asked Zack. "I think it's worth more."

The dealer looked up from the coin in his hands and smiled at Zack. "You drive a hard bargain, mister. How about seven hundred?"

"Done," said Zack.

Madison patted Zack on the back, and Zack smiled. They watched as the dealer picked up and turned each of the other coins over and over. He set the two half dollars aside, pointed to them, and said, "I'll give you eight hundred for these two coins."

Zack nodded his head. "That sounds fair."

The dealer picked up the penny and held it up, "I'll

give you a hundred fifty for this penny."

"It's in really good shape. Almost uncirculated," said Zack. "I think it's worth more."

"How 'bout two hundred?"

"Done," said Zack. "And what about this beauty?" He pointed to the 1869 S quarter—his last coin.

"This one *is* a beauty," the dealer said, as he looked up at Zack. "Better than uncirculated. Where did you get these coins?"

Without hesitation, Zack said, "In a box of my father's. My grandfather collected coins."

The dealer nodded and looked again at the quarter. "Twenty-five hundred dollars."

Madison gasped and covered her mouth with her hand.

"What? Was your boyfriend holding out on you? You didn't know these coins were worth this much?"

Madison stayed silent, and Zack said, "I couldn't part with that beauty for less than three thousand dollars."

"Yep, you drive a hard bargain. Fine. Do you have any more?"

"No, but I'd like to buy some from you. Do you have any 1840s or 1850s quarters?"

The dealer nodded and picked up the dollar tray from the counter, put it back, and placed another tray on the counter filled with quarters. "These are most of my quarters. I'm not sure of the dates."

Zack shuffled through his notes and then fingered through the coins in the tray. He'd pick them up, check the date, turn the coin over like he was checking its condition, and if it met with his approval, he'd set it to the side. When he finished he had twenty-five quarters stacked up beside the tray. He looked at Madison.

"This isn't enough," said Zack. Madison grimaced and nodded. To the dealer, Zack said, "Do you have any 1840s or 1850s half dollars?"

"I have plenty of those, some aren't in very good condition, though. Definitely not as good a condition as these that you had." He pulled out a large tray and laid it on the counter. "How about these?"

Zack looked at the coins without saying anything, while Madison watched. Before he picked any of them up, he pulled out his notes, shuffled through again glancing briefly at them. Then he looked through the tray setting coins aside. When he finished he had forty-one half dollars—most of what was in the tray—set aside on the counter next to the quarters.

"How much for these?"

The dealer carefully went through each coin and wrote an amount down. When he finished, he looked up at Zack, "I'll give you these for eighteen hundred dollars."

"You know, the condition of these coins isn't that great."

The dealer, an older fellow in his mid-fifties with close-cropped hair and blue eyes, said, "Let me make a buck here, will you?"

Zack looked at him, smiled, held out his hand, and shook hands with the dealer. "Done."

The dealer scratched out more figures on the piece of paper. "Okay. I owe you forty-seven hundred dollars, minus the eighteen hundred, that's a net to you of twenty-nine hundred dollars. Do you want a check?"

"Do you have cash?"

"Cash? That's a lot of money, I doubt it. Just a minute." The dealer disappeared in the back room, and came out counting a handful of bills. "I can give you fifteen hundred in cash. I can have the rest tomorrow, if you want to come back."

"A check is okay, Zack. I can cash it for you tomorrow," said Madison.

Zack nodded his head and said, "A check is fine," to the dealer.

The dealer wrote out a check and then counted out fifteen hundred dollars into Zack's hand. Then he held out his hand again to Zack. "Zack, nice doing business with you. My name is Stan."

"Nice to meet you, Stan. This is my friend, Madison."

"Nice to meet you, pretty lady," said Stan. As Zack and Madison turned to leave, "Come back and see me again."

When they got to the door, Zack turned around. "Stan? Are there any rare coins that you would be particularly interested in? I may be able to find them for you."

"Yes! I've been looking for months for an 1893 O silver dollar. Find that one and if it's in even decent condition, it could be worth a hundred thousand or two hundred thousand dollars."

"I don't have any resources for coins after 1870. Are there any older than 1870 that you're looking for?"

"Yes, the 1795 'Silver Plug' silver dollar is also difficult or impossible to find. That one is worth a fortune."

Zack nodded his head solemnly. "I'll see what I can do."

When they settled into the car, Madison turned to Zack. "Score! Where did you learn to do that? You were amazing! Wow! I can't believe what happened in there! You were awesome!"

Zack turned to her with a little smile on his face.

"Wouldn't you like to know, pretty lady?" Then he squeezed her hand. "Let's go home. I feel great!"

He wasn't sure if he should have squeezed her hand like that, but she had smiled and hadn't pulled away. Maybe he should have kissed her instead. That thought would have to wait for later. Right now, he couldn't be happier. Everything was going as he wanted. Now he had enough money to buy Echo back and to board him for a short time. But twenty-six dollars from his time would not last long and would not allow him to put the rest of his plan into motion. How could he get more of the old time money? Madison had said there was another coin shop in town. That might be the answer.

CHAPTER TWENTY

WHEN THEY ARRIVED home, Madison couldn't stop gushing over how magnificent Zack was. She thought maybe he was getting tired of hearing it, but he kept smiling. "You handled it so beautifully, Zack! You did everything right!"

"I did my research, and that made all the difference," said Zack. "It wouldn't have gone that way, if I hadn't known what they were worth."

"You were awesome! When you said that you wanted to be a lawyer, I honestly didn't think it was possible because you were so quiet and polite. But in there—you were—you were absolutely dynamic! You'd make a great lawyer!"

"I know I would," said Zack. "I know I would. But I need more nineteenth-century money. Can we go to the other coin store you mentioned—to see if they have more coins that I can buy?"

"That store closes at five o'clock, and I don't get off work until five o'clock."

"Can I walk there?"

"It's pretty far. We'll see what Mom says about walking that far. Or maybe she can drop you off or something. We'll work something out! You want to watch a movie tonight?"

They watched a movie, but Madison had to keep putting it on pause so she could tell him again how great he did. Zack smiled at her indulgently each time, and then pointed toward the TV, wanting the movie to continue. She wanted so much to hug him, but felt afraid she might scare him off. But he had squeezed her hand. Was that a friendly squeeze or a girlfriend squeeze? She didn't know.

The following morning her mother called to say that if Zack was feeling good, she would skip stopping by because she had an early client. Zack said he felt great and the arm felt great, so it was all good. When Madison asked her mom if Zack could walk all the way to town, Mom had said she'd prefer to check him again before he tried that long walk. Although Zack was disappointed, Madison thought he took the news well.

At work, Madison dreamed the day away. Although she was busy all day typing and filing, her mind and imagination ran free. Zack dominated her thoughts. At first going over every detail from the day before and remembering how incredibly he had handled himself, and second imagining them together, living together, studying together, and enjoying each other. She still couldn't get over the difference she had seen in him at the coin store. He had been subtle, but firm, naturally knowing when to back off and when to push forward. It was such a different view of the man she had known him to be, that it surprised her completely. In a pleasant way. A *very* pleasant way. As the day wore on and thoughts of Zack persisted, she realized the inevitable had happened.

She was in love with Zack Murphy. All her caution about falling for someone from the past had gone unheeded. There she was, hopelessly in love. And she still didn't know if he felt the same way.

Deciding she would be optimistic, she began to plan their future. First, she had to convince him to move to the future. There was no way she could live in the past. Of that she was certain. And Zack would do wonderfully here. He had already proven how easily he fit in. Imagine him in a court room! Madison sighed. She was jumping a little too far ahead here. Zack didn't even have a high school diploma. He'd have to go through four years of college and then law school. He had a lot of hard work in front of him if that's truly what he wanted. Maybe when he realized how much work it would be, he would change his mind. She wouldn't mind if he decided not to become a lawyer—although it would be nicer if he still wanted to.

But how could she approach Zack about staying in the future with her? Reminding herself that she still didn't know if he had the same feelings about her, she sighed again and leaned back in her chair. She would take it one step at a time. And the first step was to find out about Zack's feelings.

When she arrived home that evening, Madison felt strangely distant toward Zack. She had gone over and over it in her mind, and she didn't know what to do. "I like you, do you like me?" It sounded like something a first grader might say. Finding out if someone liked you was easier to think about than to put into motion. She wished Zack would just pull her into his arms and kiss her—or that she had the nerve to pull him into her arms and kiss him.

After spending the evening together watching another movie and talking, Madison turned off the television and sighed. "Time to go to sleep," she said.

"I'm tired," said Zack.

They walked into the hallway, and as they were about to part to go to their rooms, they turned toward each other. Did she have the nerve to just grab him and kiss him? Her eyes got wide, and she held her breath—but no. She didn't have the nerve. Had she seen Zack's arms move almost imperceptibly toward her? If they did, that's all the farther they got. Maybe he didn't have the nerve either. How would they ever get together if they were both too afraid to show their feelings?

CHAPTER TWENTY-ONE

THEY WERE SO close! They had both turned to face each other at the same time, and there was the opportunity, but he didn't have the confidence to just wrap his arms around her and kiss her. His arms wanted to—they had started moving in that direction, but he consciously made the effort to stop. He couldn't carry through. He could, he reminded himself, haggle with someone in another century, but he couldn't kiss the woman of his dreams. How did he ever expect to get anywhere in life, if he didn't have the nerve to move forward with Madison? As much as he wanted to be a lawyer, nothing else mattered if he couldn't be with her.

Because he felt so disappointed in himself for not kissing Madison, he slept fitfully that night and awoke feeling tired. At breakfast, Zack was about to take Madison's hand and tell her how he felt when Kat came through the doorway.

"How's my favorite patient this morning?"

Zack smiled at her. "I'm doing great, Kat, thank you."

She walked over and put her hand on his forehead. "Feels normal, let's check to be sure." She took the thermometer out of her bag and ran it across his forehead. "Yup, normal. Let's see the wound." Kat examined the wound, pressing her fingers on the surrounding area. "Any soreness?"

"Almost completely gone," said Zack.

"You're doing great," said Kat. "You have responded well to the penicillin, and your wound is now healing properly, no thanks to that quack you call a doctor. I think, Zack, that I'm going to give you a clean bill of health. You can return to the past anytime."

"I'll take him back Saturday, Mom. I've been wanting to visit Granny anyway."

"Sure. That sounds great, if you don't mind staying here another few days, Zack."

Zack smiled and gave a quick glance toward Madison. "No, I'm having a great time here. I don't mind staying."

"Sounds good. You're welcome to ride my horse back there, Zack. Madison can pony her home, and she'll be fine. She's a good horse. You can ride, can't you?"

"Yes, Ma'am. I used to have my own horse, and thanks to the coin dealer yesterday, I'm going to buy him back when I go home." Zack caught himself too late. He didn't want to call the past home.

"Oh, Mom, can you drop Zack off at the other coin dealer?"

"Sorry, Zack, I have another early appointment, and I have to hurry as it is. Why can't you drop him off, Madison?"

"It's on Pioneer—the other side of town," said Madison.

"Isn't there one on Sixth Street?" Kat asked. "You could walk to that one, Zack. Pioneer is way too far to walk to, though."

"We've already been to that one, Mom. Zack needs to get more 1800s money so he can board his horse, and he already bought all the coins he could from the one on Sixth."

"Well, you two kids work it out. I need to get to work. Bye, love." Kat waved as she hurried out the door.

"Sorry, Zack. Maybe I can hurry home tomorrow at lunch and give you a ride."

"Okay."

"I need to leave right now, though. Have a good day. See you soon." Madison put her hand on his shoulder as she walked by.

She liked him! He knew she did! Now he just needed the courage to either tell her how he felt, kiss her, or both. It all scared him. Zack knew why he was so skeery. He had never kissed a girl before. Sad truth was that he had never met one that he wanted to. It didn't matter now—he wanted to kiss Madison, and he had to find a way to make it happen.

After she left, he started a Google search on bookstores. He needed to buy books on studying for the GED test. That was his first step to moving to the future—although he didn't consider it the future anymore—he considered it his time. When he looked online how to get to one bookstore, it turned out to be close to the coin dealer they had been to, so he knew how to get there. Perfect. And Kat had said it was all right for him to walk there. Then he looked up where the other coin dealer was. According to the map, it was miles away from the first one. He hoped that he could get to it before he went back Saturday. If he couldn't, it would ruin his plans.

Zack spent the morning on the internet. At noon, he made himself a sandwich for lunch, then put a list of books in his pocket, and left the house. He had decided to bring his Pennsylvania law book with him. Although he didn't know if they bought old books at bookstores, he thought it was worth a try.

It only took him fifteen minutes to walk to the bookstore. When he walked in and saw all the books there, he gasped. He had never seen so many books in one place before. Walking up to the counter, he waited until the clerk had finished helping another person, and then he approached him. "Hallo, I was wondering if you would be interested in buying this book."

"We don't sell any used books here, but can I see it?" Zack handed him the book. "*Purdon's Digest of Laws of Pennsylvani*a. It's old and in good condition. Wow, it was published in 1837. Dude! You could sell this on eBay and make a fortune! Would you mind if I looked at it while you look around?"

"No, go ahead. Where are the books on the GED test?"

"Straight down this aisle, turn left at the end and they're on the bottom shelf."

"Thanks," said Zack, as he walked down the aisle. He didn't want to ask the guy what eBay was—he could ask Madison when she got home, or look it up on the internet. The bottom shelf had many books on it, and before long, Zack had picked out seven books. He wanted to get a separate book for each subject he'd be tested on, a book that had *all* the subjects in it, a book that included test taking strategies, and a book of practice tests.

Before returning to the counter to pay for the books, he decided to walk up and down each aisle looking at the books. The sheer quantity of them amazed him. When he walked past the section on coin collecting, he looked through the books and picked out the one he wanted that he had seen mentioned on the internet. Since he couldn't look anything up on the computer while he was in the old Red Bluff, the book would be perfect. As he walked back to the front counter, he noticed a display with a book called *Sycamore Row* by John Grisham. Since he was enjoying *A Time to Kill* so much, he picked it up and was delighted to find that it was the sequel. Adding that to his stack, he plopped all the books on the front counter.

"I checked out this book for you. It could be worth a lot of money, just sayin'."

"Cool, thanks," said Zack.

The clerk rang up all the books and put them into two plastic sacks. "Someone's studying for the GED test," said the clerk, grinning. "When are they taking it?"

"When? What do you mean when?"

"Oh, it's only given at certain times of the year."

Zack's heart sank. What if he couldn't take the test in time to enroll in college? As Zack handed the clerk the money, he said, "Oh, I didn't realize that. Listen, I have a long way to walk, is there something besides a bag for me to carry the books in?"

"How about a backpack? You can pick up one at the thrift store down the street for a song."

Zack didn't know what he meant by song, but he asked, "Which way?" When the clerk pointed toward the right, Zack said, "Could you keep the books here for me while I walk down there?"

"Sure, dude. No problem."

Zack wasn't sure what a backpack was, but he thought that Madison might have mentioned it during one of their conversations. Walking down the street toward the thrift store, whatever that was, Zack looked around him and marveled at all the stores. One after another after another. He'd never seen anything like it. The mountains —the same mountains he could see surrounding the old Red Bluff—still guarded the town. Maybe that's why he felt so at home here—because it really was home. What's a hundred years? Meaningless.

He laughed and then found himself in front of the thrift store. Walking in, he looked around and noticed that most of the clothes he saw didn't look new. When he found the clerk, he asked her about backpacks, and she showed him where to look. He picked them all up and inspected each one carefully. One was too dirty, one too big, one had a broken zipper, and then he found the right one—perfect for what he needed. After looking over the rest of the store to see what they had, he paid the clerk and walked back to the bookstore.

After he put the books, including his Pennsylvania law book, into the backpack, he thanked the clerk, pulled the backpack on, and left the store. Smiling, he walked slowly back to the house, taking in all the newnesses of the century. The cars never ceased to amaze him, and he finally saw what Madison had described as an "eighteen-wheeler." He counted the wheels as it drove by, and sure enough, it had eighteen of them. Wow! No one in the old Red Bluff could ever imagine anything like that. There were so many amazing things to experience about the twenty-first century, and Zack had only just arrived. He loved this century and loved the idea of living in it.

As he walked back, he wondered what time it was. He hoped that he would get home before Madison, so he could greet her when she came through the door. She liked that, so Zack liked doing it for her. When he arrived back at the house, a surprise was waiting for him when he opened the door.

CHAPTER TWENTY-TWO

MADISON SPENT ALMOST the entire morning in court. At ten o'clock, Marcus, the owner of the law firm, had come in and asked her to take a special message to an attorney in court and wait for the answer. That didn't happen often, so Madison felt pleased that he had asked her. She always liked going into court—it made her feel like she was part of the legal system, and she liked that. After Madison gave the attorney the message, he nodded, and she walked to the back of the courtroom to sit and wait. The attorney knew it needed a response, but he was in the middle of a trial. She had to wait for the next recess. That was fine. Madison loved watching a good attorney work, and she knew this guy was good.

Two hours later, after one witness was brought to tears, and left the entire jury gasping, the judge finally called a recess. The attorney stood up, looked quickly around the room for her, spotted her, and quickly walked over. He scribbled a reply to the note and gave it to Madison. She thanked him and drove back to the office.

After handing the note personally to Marcus, she grabbed her lunch and hurried to the lunchroom. It was late, and she was starved. Several other women ate late lunches, too, so the talk in the room was animated. Between law office gossip, men, and speculations about law school, there was never a lack for conversation.

Madison hadn't mentioned her feelings about Zack to anyone. What she felt for him seemed more special than something shared with casual acquaintances over lunch. So she listened quietly, joining in the conversation only occasionally.

When she got back into her office and started typing, she realized that besides brief instances, she hadn't given Zack much thought all day. Not that she had time—but it made her realize how often she normally thought about him. *All* the time. She realized that she had thought about him long enough. It was time to do something about it! Whether he felt the same way about her or not, she needed to find out. In her heart, she felt strongly that he did feel the same way. But her head kept giving her reasons for doubt. Regardless, something had to be done. She had to find out one way or the other.

So what should she do? Should she speak to him about it, or just grab him, kiss him, and see if he kissed back? If she kissed him, and he didn't feel the same way, she would lose his friendship. And his friendship was important to her. She enjoyed his humor and both sides of his personality—his quiet demeanor and the enterprising side of him that she had seen at the coin store. Zack would make a wonderful study partner—bright and perceptive. That is, if he lived in her time and still wanted to become a lawyer. Maybe kissing him wasn't the way to proceed.

Deciding that talking to him would be better, Madison set about figuring out what to say. Again the first idea she came up with, "I like you, do you like me?" sounded way too first-grader for her. "I have feelings for you"? That sounded too heavy, it might scare him off. "I kinda like you"? Too wishy-washy. "I think you're handsome and smart, and I like you," could be something you'd say to a friend. Or maybe come at it from a different angle. "You said you wanted to be a lawyer—would you want to be one in this century?" But why would that mean that she liked him? It really didn't.

The first grader comment and question kept coming back to her. That must mean something. Maybe she could just tweak it a little. How about, "I like you, Zack. I mean I *really* like you." It sounded good. And she could touch his hand as she said it, and maybe raise her eyebrows. No. Nix on the eyebrows. That was too suggestive. A touch of the hand would be perfect.

That was it. She had decided. When she arrived home, after they had dinner and were sitting around talking—before she put on a movie—she would move closer to him on the couch, touch his hand, and just say it. Now that she had decided, she could hardly wait to get home. And get it over with, if she had to admit the truth.

Someone walking briskly into her office interrupted Madison's thoughts. It was Marcus, holding up hangers with suits on them.

"Madison, I need you to drop these off after work. Put a rush on them, and then pick them up first thing in the morning."

Madison glanced at the clock on the wall above the door. It was five minutes before five o'clock. "I'm sorry, Marcus. I need to go straight home tonight, so I can't do that. Someone is waiting for me."

Marcus blinked his eyes and rotated back on his heels. "You what?"

Madison didn't want to lose her job over this, but she didn't want to do it, either. She knew that Sarah used to take care of his cleaning all the time, but Sarah made a lot more money than she did. And Madison had no intention of becoming his dry cleaning go-to-girl. "I said I can't do it. I have someone waiting for me, and I need to get right home." Madison stood up, logged out of her computer, and grabbed her purse. "I need to leave right away, and I can't do it. Sorry, Marcus."

"Oh, well, okay then. I'll find somebody else. Sorry to have bothered you," said Marcus, practically stumbling over his words. Not many people said no to Marcus. Regardless, Madison wasn't going to say yes to this favor that would undoubtedly become a habit. She wanted none of it.

CHAPTER TWENTY-THREE

WHEN ZACK OPENED the door to the house, he heard the television. Turning, he looked out the front window to check if Madison's car was out there. It wasn't. Two dogs met him at the door. They looked like Jet and Bingo, Jenna's and Josiah's dogs. So when he walked into the living room, he wasn't surprised to see Josiah sitting on the couch, holding the remote, and watching television.

"Josiah! What are you doing here?"

Josiah adjusted the volume on the TV and turned to look at him. With a big grin on his face, Josiah said, "Looking for *you*, Zack! We thought you'd be in bed, recuperating. What are you doing up and around?"

"I healed fast. Kat gave me a clean bill of health this morning. I just walked to the bookstore and bought some books."

"Oh, that's good." Josiah moved his head toward the doorway. "Jenna! Zack's here! No need to worry!" Then to Zack, "You know women, Zack. She was worried about you."

"Where is Jenna?"

"She's in our room. Do you know which bedroom that

is? Go down the hallway and before you get to Madison's room, there's a door on the right. Go see her. It will make her feel better," said Josiah, as he adjusted the volume back up and turned back to the TV.

Zack walked through the doorway. He had never been down the hallway past his bathroom. He turned left and followed Josiah's instructions. The door was open. Jenna sat in front of a big screen that must be a big computer. Before this, he had only seen Madison's laptop computer. From the doorway, he said, "Hi, Jenna. I'm fine."

Jenna turned around with a big smile on her face. "Zack! So good to see you up and feeling better. Sarah and Matthew have been very worried about you. And since Josiah and I were coming to town anyway, today, I told her I'd check on you. It doesn't hurt that we're all in the same house, huh?" She laughed, and Zack joined her.

"I'm doing great. Kat gave me a clean bill of health this morning."

"Oh, good. We're riding back tomorrow. Would you like to come with us?"

"Oh, um, actually, Madison is going to take me Saturday. She wanted to see Granny." And then, to make sure Jenna understood, "I don't mind waiting for Saturday. I like it here."

"Okay," said Jenna, turning back to the computer. "Glad you're doing well, Zack."

Zack walked back to the living room and found Madison home and talking to Josiah. His first reaction was a sharp dose of jealousy—until he realized it was Josiah and Madison. Josiah, newly married and heels over head in love with Jenna, would never flirt with another woman. He wasn't that kind of man. And Madison would not flirt with her Aunt Jenna's husband. Although he didn't know Madison that well except for the past week, he knew she wasn't that kind of woman. Zack pushed aside the unreasonable feelings of jealousy and entered the living room.

"Hi, Madison!"

"Hi, Zack. Josiah just invited you and me to dinner with him and Jenna at the Thai restaurant. Would you like to go?"

"Sure. What's tie?"

"You'll find out! You'll love it! Honestly, you've been here all week, and I never even thought to take you out on the town." She looked at Josiah. "Poor Zack had to eat my cooking all week."

"I enjoy your cooking, Madison, and enjoy helping you."

"You're just saying that to be nice, Zack."

Jenna entered the room and said, "Hi, Madison. Josiah, did you ask them?"

"Yes, and they want to go. Shall we leave now?"

"Sure," said Jenna. "You guys ready to go?"

Zack and Madison both said yes. The two couples walked outside.

"I'll go get the truck," said Josiah.

"Josiah's going to drive?" asked Zack.

"I taught him," said Jenna. "He'd been wanting to learn. I finally broke down, took him to a parking lot, and showed him. He's a pretty good driver. You don't have to worry, Zack."

"I wasn't worried, just surprised."

When Josiah drove the truck up to them, Jenna said, "Zack, why don't you sit in the front with Josiah. Madison and I can sit in the back."

"Okay." Zack climbed into the front seat. He noticed that it was much higher than a car, which he could just step into. As they drove to town, Zack thought it felt different from riding in a car, too. Josiah impressed him by doing everything right. Zack wondered if maybe he could learn to drive, too. Maybe Madison would teach him after he moved to the future. *If* he moved to the future.

Josiah parked behind the Thai restaurant. They walked in, and Zack looked around at all the elephants in the room. There were pictures of elephants, stone statues of elephants, and elephants with sparkly things on their bodies. Pictures of people in clothing he didn't recognize and other statues adorned the room, also. Zack grinned. "This is awesome!"

Jenna and Madison laughed. Josiah didn't get it. "Awesome!" said Madison. "Zack, you're becoming absolutely twenty-first-century! Soon, we're not going to let you go back!"

They were seated in a corner and given water and menus. Zack had a seat where he could see everything. "This is so amazing. It's nothing like the restaurant at the hotel."

"That much is true," said Josiah. "Now you know why we come here once or twice a month!"

"You do? I can see why. This place is so cool. I love it," said Zack. He kept looking around and marveling at all the unfamiliar sights.

"Zack, look at the menu. I'm starved. We need to order. You can look around later!" said Jenna.

"Okay," said Zack. Looking at the menu, he read each item. Many words were not familiar. He decided that he would make the same choice as Madison, so he closed the menu.

"Oh, I know they have pineapple chicken, but I can't find it," said Madison.

"It's the third item from the bottom on the right-hand page," said Zack.

Madison looked up at Zack and then down at the menu. "Yep, there it is, thanks, Zack. Do they have any desserts?"

"Yes," Zack said. "Three items on the back."

While Madison turned the menu over to look at the dessert menu, Jenna tilted her head and looked at Zack. "Zack, what are the dessert items?"

"Fried bananas, Thai coconut custard, and mango pudding."

"Zack! Wow! You have a photographic memory!" said Jenna.

"What's that?" asked Zack.

"It means you look at something once and remember exactly what you saw."

"Can't everybody do that?" asked Zack.

"No! Not many people can," said Jenna.

Then the waitress walked up to their table and took their orders. Madison ordered the pineapple chicken, as did Zack, and Josiah and Jenna ordered something called Pad Thai. Zack didn't know what that was.

When the waitress left, Jenna said, "Zack, what have you been doing since you got here—besides recuperating?"

"I've been on the computer a lot, researching coins. Then Madison and I drove to the coin dealer, and I sold some coins and bought some more from the nineteenth century."

"You should have seen him at the coin dealer! You

know how quiet and polite Zack is? Well at the coin dealer, he was absolutely dynamic! You should have seen him."

"Oh, I wasn't really that brilliant," said Zack.

"Yes, you were! He was awesome!"

"So you made some money, Zack. What are you going to do with it?" asked Josiah.

"Buy back my horse," said Zack.

"I didn't know you had a horse," said Josiah.

"Yeah, I had to sell him before you came to town. But I need more money to board him."

"Zack needs to go to the other coin dealer, the one on Pioneer, so he can get more nineteenth-century money," said Madison. "We bought out all the coins that Zack wanted from the dealer on Sixth Street. And I haven't been able to take him to the other place."

"We can take you tomorrow, Zack, before we return. But you can ask the guy on Sixth to order more for you. That's what Sarah and I did. Maybe the other place can do that, too," said Jenna.

"You really should have seen him, though," said Madison. "He knew what each coin was worth. He sold his coins at the highest price, and then bought the cheapest nineteenth-century coins."

Josiah reached into his pocket, pulled out some coins, and put them on the table in front of Zack. "What about these, Zack?"

Zack looked over the coins and then picked up one quarter and turned it over. "1869 S. I sold one just like this for three thousand dollars. But this one is in better condition."

"Three thousand dollars for a quarter? And we've been getting only fifteen hundred for the gold dollars that we sell!" said Jenna. She picked up the quarter, looked at it, and handed it back to Zack. "Amazing."

Zack gathered up the coins and handed them all back to Josiah. Then Josiah looked through them and said, "Is this the quarter you mentioned?"

"Yes, that's the one. You can get more than three thousand for it, I'm sure," said Zack.

"No," said Josiah, as he handed it back to Zack. "*You* can."

"I can't take that from you. It's worth too much," said Zack.

"No, Zack. It's worth a quarter to me. That's all. I'm giving you a quarter."

"I can't accept it." Zack tried to hand the quarter back to Josiah.

"I'll tell you what, Zack. You give me a quarter for it. Then, we'll be even."

Jenna reached across the table and patted Zack's hand. "It's okay, Zack. You take it. Just give us a quarter. It's fine."

Madison said, "Zack. They want to trade you a quarter for a quarter. Do it!"

Reluctantly, Zack reached in his pocket, took out a shiny 2012 quarter, and handed it to Josiah. "Here."

"Thank you, Zack. Good deal," said Josiah, as he shook Zack's hand.

Zack still felt unsure about what had just happened. He looked at Josiah seriously. "Okay, Josiah, a quarter for a quarter, but I'm buying you supper." Smiling then, he said, "I have plenty of twenty-first-century money!"

Madison said, "He does! I still owe him more than a thousand dollars!"

The waitress came and placed the plates in front of

them. Zack thought the smells were intoxicating. He had never smelled anything like them. When he looked down at what he ordered, he didn't know what to do. "Madison?"

"You weren't expecting that, were you, Zack? It's a pineapple. Just use your fork and eat out of it like it was a bowl."

"What is it?" asked Zack. In front of Zack was a pineapple sliced down the middle. The inside of the fruit had been removed and replaced with chicken, chunks of pineapple, tiny ears of corn like he'd never seen before, and other items that tasted delicious but he didn't know what they were.

After they had finished eating and ordering dessert, Madison excused herself to go to the bathroom. When she walked away, Josiah said, "So how do you like it here in the future, Zack?"

"I love it here, Josiah. I don't want to leave."

"Does Madison know that?" Jenna dabbed her mouth with her napkin and looked at Zack.

"She's part of the reason I don't want to leave. But, no, she doesn't know."

"What would you do in this century?" asked Josiah.

"I want to be a lawyer."

"You know, I was a lawyer here, Zack. It takes a lot of schooling. Do you have a high school diploma?" asked Jenna.

"I didn't know you were a lawyer, Jenna. No, I don't have a diploma. But I can get a GED. Today, I bought a bunch of books so I can study for the test. But the guy at the bookstore said they only give the test at certain times."

"Late last year, I read something that in 2014, they

were starting on computerized testing, and you could take the tests any time," said Jenna. "You know there are several subjects. But you can take the different parts of the test at different times. There is probably more than one site in Red Bluff where you can take the tests."

"I bought a separate book for each subject," said Zack. "I like to be prepared, and I don't want to take any chance on not passing."

Jenna put her hand on Zack's. "Zack, if you have all these plans, I think you need to talk to Madison about them."

Zack nodded at her, as Madison returned from the bathroom and sat down.

"Jenna," said Madison, smiling, "you're not going to believe what happened today with Marcus! He asked me to take his dry cleaning, and I said no!"

Jenna laughed. "Sarah was stuck doing that job, and for a long time she liked it. She thought it meant that Marcus trusted her."

"I figured it would get to be a habit—him pawning off his laundry on me. And I wasn't going to let that get started. I'm not his maid!"

"Well, don't worry about him firing you or anything. He won't."

"Firing me?" Madison laughed. "It surprised him so much he didn't know what to say!"

Jenna reached across the table and patted Madison's hand. "Good show, Madison. Good job in standing up for yourself!"

"Thanks, Jenna!"

Zack looked at Madison with pride. He wanted to say, "You're awesome, Madison," but he just smiled at her instead.

CHAPTER TWENTY-FOUR

THE FOLLOWING MORNING, Zack was in the living room working on Madison's computer when he heard Josiah walk down the hallway and knock on Zack's partially closed bedroom door. "C'mon, Zack! Up and at 'em! We need to go back to Red Bluff early, so if you want to go to the coin dealer, better get up and ready now."

"Josiah!" Zack called out. "I'm in here. I'm dressed, and I've already eaten breakfast."

Josiah stepped through the doorway with a smile on his face. "Already hooked on the internet, Zack? You really *do* belong in the twenty-first century! Except for the Thai restaurant and the ice cream here, I can't wait to get home!" Josiah disappeared from Zack's view for an instant, then Zack heard him say, "He's already up, Jenna. C'mon. Let's go. I want to get home."

Seconds later, Josiah walked back out to the living room, followed by Jenna. "Good morning, Zack!" said Jenna. "I see that Madison already has you hooked on the internet."

"Morning, Jenna. I like to look stuff up. That's all. I'm learning a lot," said Zack.

"Would you like to have breakfast with us? I can fix you some eggs," said Jenna.

"Thank you, Jenna. Madison fixed some eggs, so I've already eaten."

Jenna smiled at him and walked to the kitchen with Josiah. While Zack worked on the computer, he could hear them in the kitchen, plugging in the coffee maker, using the toaster, and making eggs. Zack stopped what he was doing to listen to them. He wasn't eavesdropping. He enjoyed the easy way they were with each other—gentle conversation interspersed with laughter—it was the kind of relationship he hoped to have someday with Madison. Reluctantly, he returned his attention to the computer.

An hour later, Josiah and Jenna emerged from the kitchen. "Sorry it took us so long, Zack. We get carried away with our conversations like that," said Josiah.

Zack smiled. "I'm in no hurry, Josiah. But someday I hope to have the kind of relationship that you and Jenna have."

Josiah pulled Jenna into him. "If you do, boy, you'll be damn lucky." Then he kissed Jenna on her forehead. Looking at Zack, he said, "You ready?"

"Sure. Let me put the laptop back in Madison's room. I'll only be a second."

A few minutes later, the three of them walked outside. "Do you want to drive in the car or the truck today, Zack?" asked Josiah.

"I like the truck!" said Zack.

"I'll go get it," said Josiah.

A minute later, Josiah had driven up to them. Jenna let Zack sit in the front again, and she climbed into the back seat.

"Zack, if you want, maybe I can teach you how to drive," said Josiah.

"Josiah! You just learned to drive!" said Jenna.

"Yes, but I'm a good driver. *You* told me that."

"Okay, well, you are and I did, but I'm not sure if Zack is ready for that. He's only been in a car a few times."

"Oh, c'mon, Jenna. I'm a quick learner," said Zack.

"Maybe another time, Zack. Today we need to get back to town," said Jenna.

Josiah shrugged his shoulders. "Sorry, Zack, I tried." Then Zack and Josiah spoke about different vehicles, and Josiah suggested several for Zack to look at.

Jenna huffed playfully in the back seat. "Men and their vehicles!"

After several minutes of driving, during which Josiah talked Zack into buying a car after he moved to the new Red Bluff, they arrived at the other coin dealer. Josiah parked in the parking lot, and the three of them walked into the store together.

Zack walked up to the counter and pulled the quarter out of his pocket. "Are you interested in buying this coin? It's in really good shape."

An older woman, even older than Eliza, picked up the coin and held it under a lighted magnifier. "This is beautiful! I've never seen one in such good condition." She turned it over and kept looking. "Hardly any blemishes. It looks almost like it was just minted. It's not proof, but it's close." She looked up with a hint of a smile on her face. "Oh! I shouldn't have told you how wonderful it was. Now you'll want more for it."

Zack smiled back. "Whatever's fair, ma'am."

"Oh, such a polite boy. I'm going to like doing business with you." She patted his hand. "What would you think about forty-five hundred dollars?"

Zack blinked, gulped, and coughed out his reply. "Ah, yeah," he said with a smile. He heard Jenna gasp at the counter next to him, but Josiah stayed silent.

"Do you have any more that you'd like to sell?" asked the woman, cradling her new quarter to her chest.

"No, but I'm interested in buying some. Do you have any 1840s or 1850s quarters or half dollars?"

"Sure thing!" said the woman. She turned around and put two trays on the counter. "I don't think any of them are as good as the one you just sold me, though."

"That's okay," said Zack, as he examined the coins. "Poor condition is fine." He started picking out quarters and setting them aside. Then he picked out several half dollars. When he finished, he had found thirty-four half dollars and thirty-four quarters. "How much for these?" asked Zack, as he looked up at the woman.

"Let me see," she said, as she wrote some figures down on a pad of paper by the register. Nodding her head, she looked at the coins again, scratched out some more figures and looked up. She squinted her eyes at Zack. "Are you an Indian boy?" Before Zack could answer, she added, "Oh! I apologize. I know the politically correct term is now Native American, but in my day, it was Indian. Anyway, are you?"

Zack felt defensive and balled his hands into fists. He had enough of the name-calling in his time, but he didn't expect it in the twenty-first century. Madison had said things were different here. "Yes, ma'am, I am," he said as politely as he could manage.

The old woman nodded. "Yes, I thought so. Well, I'll tell you, boy, I would normally charge upwards of three thousand dollars for these coins, but since you're Indian —I mean Native American—I'll give them to you for twenty-five hundred."

Zack blinked and looked at her curiously. He had to blink his eyes repeatedly, because they were filling with tears. That was something he had never expected. He was getting something special *because* he was Indian. Zack nodded and held out his hand. "Yes, thank you, twenty-five hundred is fine. My name is Zack."

The woman shook his hand vigorously. "Hello, Zack. My name is Susan. Nice to make your acquaintance. I'm sorry about what we did to your people."

Zack couldn't look up at her, but he motioned toward Jenna and Josiah. "These are my friends, Jenna and Josiah." Zack's thoughts were swimming so fast in his head that he couldn't think a coherent thought. The room started to get blurry, and he blinked the tears from his eyes again. "Thank you very much, Susan. Good-bye."

"Zack, wait! I need to pay you," said Susan.

"You can pay my friends," said Zack, as he approached the door. As he walked out, he heard Jenna say to Susan, "It's okay. Where he's from, they make fun of him for being a Native American." And that's the last he heard before the door closed behind him.

Several minutes later, Jenna and Josiah came out to the truck where Zack was waiting outside. He had composed himself by then, and he looked up sheepishly. "Sorry."

Josiah put his hand on Zack's shoulder. "No need to be sorry, Zack. I've seen the way those men treat you in Matthew's saloon. You have nothing to be sorry about at all. It is good for a man to cry. It shows he has heart."

Josiah tapped him on the chest. "C'mon, get in. Jenna and I need to get back."

When they all got into the truck, Jenna said, "Zack, she gave us a check for two thousand dollars. Do you need it right away? We can stop at the bank on the way home if you want."

"No, Jenna, thank you. Whenever it is convenient for you. What I needed was more nineteenth-century money, and I got that. Oh, do you have it?"

"Yes, right here," said Jenna.

"I should give you back some money, anyway. I didn't expect her to pay me so much for that coin."

"We made a fair trade, Zack. I gave you a quarter, you gave me a quarter. We're even. The money belongs to you," said Josiah.

Zack nodded his head. "Okay."

"You did seem surprised when she said 'forty-five hundred dollars.'"

"That's more than the other guy would have paid me, I think. But she charged more for the old coins," said Zack.

"Then you know what you have to do, Zack," said Jenna.

Zack turned around and smiled into the back seat at Jenna. "Sell her my nineteenth-century coins, and buy more coins at the other place!"

"Exactly!" said Jenna.

"I really liked Stan—the guy at the first place. But I really like Susan, also. People here are so nice!"

"Not all of them, Zack. But most are."

"I belong here," said Zack. "Jenna, Josiah," as he said their names, he looked at them, "you know I do."

CHAPTER TWENTY-FIVE

TWO DAYS FLEW by. Madison was busy at work doing special projects with no time to think about what she would do about Zack. She spent most of Thursday night on the phone with a friend whose boyfriend had just broken up with her. Friday night, she had dinner with that friend, so Madison still did not have a chance to talk to Zack.

Next she knew it was late Saturday afternoon, and she and Zack were getting ready to ride back to the old Red Bluff. She noticed that he had a backpack that was full of books. When she asked what he'd bought, he showed her a coin book and the latest John Grisham. But she thought he was trying to hide something from her. Books? What was there to hide? It didn't seem important enough to concern herself with. Her main focus now was to check into the hotel and find Granny to talk to her about Zack.

When they arrived at the cave, Madison noticed that Zack was getting antsy. "I want to get off and look around," he said.

"Not now, Zack. I really want to see Granny. Do you

mind?" Madison knew that the first time Zack came through the cave, he was in the wagon with his eyes closed, barely conscious. But she hoped he wouldn't mind. He could still see much of the cave from horseback as they walked through.

"No, it's okay," said Zack. "I'll see it another time."

Madison wondered what he meant. It sounded like he planned to return to the future. To her? With her? Now wasn't the time to talk to him about it.

When they emerged from the cave and trotted onto the main road, Zack smiled when he saw the sign that said Red Bluff, Colorado. "I recognize that sign!"

"We're almost there," said Madison. "Would you mind taking the horses to the livery while I check in?"

"No, not at all. That way I can buy Echo right away. I don't want another day to go by without him. Then I'll go to the saloon to see Matthew and Sarah. Will you meet me there later, or will you spend the whole evening with Granny, too?"

"I'll meet you over there sometime," said Madison. "Here we are." After dismounting, she handed the reins to Zack. "See you later, Zack."

"Bye, Madison!"

As Zack rode down the street leading Chaco, Madison stood in front of the hotel, watching. She smiled when he reached the end of the block and turned his head to look back at her and wave. Madison sighed. She was hopelessly in love with him and didn't know how he felt about her. What a miserable situation, she thought.

When she walked into the hotel, Eliza greeted her. "Hello, Madison! Nice to see you again. Have you come to return our young Zack?"

Eliza was warm and friendly, and Madison liked her a

lot. With her husband, Samuel, Eliza owned the hotel. And Granny and her new husband, Edward, lived here. Edward was Eliza's father. It was all one big happy family, and Madison was happy to be a part of it. Eliza always treated Madison like family, and Madison appreciated that.

"Yes, Zack is back, and I also wanted to spend some time with Granny."

"She's around here somewhere—maybe in her room, though—because my father is in the restaurant with Samuel."

"Okay, I'll find her," said Madison. Eliza gave her the key, and Madison walked upstairs to her room. Since Granny had married Edward, Eliza had stopped charging Madison when she stayed at the hotel. At first, Madison had protested. But when Eliza insisted, Madison gave in. After all, they were family now. Edward was officially her great-grandfather, which made Eliza her grandmother. Since Madison had lost her maternal grandparents in the barn fire and she never knew her paternal grandparents, she liked the idea of having Eliza and Samuel in her life. They were both such wonderful people.

She put her backpack in her room and walked down the hallway to Granny and Edward's room. When Granny opened the door, Madison hugged her. "Granny, I've missed you so much!"

"I've missed you, too, Madison. You never call, you never write," said Granny in her mock angry voice.

Madison laughed. "I would if I could, Granny. I would if I could."

"Come on in to my humble abode. Sit down there, make yourself as comfortable as you can with this crummy furniture."

"Granny, the furniture is fine, and you could get new furniture if you wanted!"

"Who needs new furniture? My butt won't get any younger sitting on newer furniture! So what have you been up to? You still working for those crooked attorneys?"

"Granny! They're not crooked. It's the same office that Jenna used to practice in."

"Madison. *All* attorneys are crooked in one way or another. That's why Jenna quit. Because she wasn't crooked, so she didn't fit in."

"Oh, Granny. I'm going to be a lawyer, and I'm not going to be crooked."

"Then you'll be the first!" said Granny.

Madison wanted to change the subject. Besides Granny's acerbic way of speaking, she could be intolerably stubborn. "How do you like living here—you know, in the past?"

"It's better than living in that old folks' home in the future!"

"Granny, you didn't live in an old folks' home. You had a nice apartment." Madison looked around the small room. It had a full-size bed, two chairs, two bedside tables, a chest of drawers, and a wooden sink with a pitcher of water on it, a wood stove in one corner and a chamber pot in the other (just like Madison's hotel room). "Your apartment was bigger than *this*, Granny. You don't even have a composting toilet."

"I don't mind peeing in that vase over there. I know, I know, its proper name is a chamber pot, but it looks like a vase to me. Living in the new Red Bluff was like being in an old folks' home. What did I do all day? Gab on the phone to those few friends who hadn't kicked the bucket yet, and then what did they talk about? All their ailments. I was sick of hearing about their ailments! No one here talks about that. They just live their life and enjoy every day. How do I like living here? I love it! It's paradise for me."

"And how do you like being married again? Grampy's been gone for a long time."

"Married life? With Edward? That rotten old coot!" Granny smiled at Madison. "I love it. He treats me well, and we get along wonderfully. The old coot." Granny wiped a tear from her eye. "Now look what you've made me do! Get all sentimental! I'll lose my grouchy reputation!" Granny stood up and straightened her long dress. She winked at Madison. "And I'll tell you something else, great-granddaughter. The sex is awesome!"

CHAPTER TWENTY-SIX

As Zack led Madison's horse down the street, he smiled when he thought about how she had still been looking at him when he turned around to see if she was still there. Although he didn't know for sure, in his heart, he believed that she felt the same way. At least he hoped so.

He rode into the livery stable. "Ezra! You here?"

The lanky man appeared from the back. "What do we have here, Zack? I heard you left town—and now you come back with two horses!"

"They aren't mine, Ezra. They need to be boarded for one night. But—do you by any chance still have Echo?"

"You want to see him? You haven't been to see him in a long time—years. And I never told you this, but when you walk by and he sees you—he still nickers. Yes, he's here. I'll go get him for you."

"Ezra, I don't want to see him. I want to buy him back. Will you sell him to me?"

"I knew you'd be back for him someday! Many people offered to buy him—such a pretty boy with a good temperament—and I always said no. Zack, I've seen people with horses before, but you and Echo had a bond that I hadn't seen before. And by the way, I only rented him out enough to pay his board—and then only to people who I knew would be kind to him."

Tears came to Zack's eyes. "Ezra, thank you. Thank you so much," he said, as he turned away.

"Let me take these two and get them settled before I bring Echo out. You two need some time alone." Ezra took the reins of the two horses and led them to stalls in the back.

A minute later, another stall opened and a black and white pinto stepped out. He turned toward Zack, nickered, and loped up to him, almost pushing him over. Zack stroked the horse, whispering to him how much he loved and missed him, and told him they'd never be apart again.

Several minutes later, Ezra walked up from the back with a bridle and handed it to Zack. "See, horses never forget. And I knew this horse would never forget you. Here's your bridle, Zack. I saved it for you. It's only been used on Echo."

"Thanks so much, Ezra—for everything. How much do you want for him?"

"Let's see, now. What did I give you for him? Seven dollars? Yes, I believe it was. Seven dollars it is, then."

"Shouldn't it be more?" asked Zack.

"I told you; I rented him out enough to pay his board. As far as I'm concerned, you've been boarding him all this time. Really, I shouldn't charge you anything."

Zack pulled some coins from his pocket. "Ezra, here's fifteen dollars. I'd appreciate it if you'd keep that. Everything you've done for him—and for me—you deserve more. I can't thank you enough."

"If it means that much to you, Zack. But as I told you,

the connection between you two was easy enough to see."

"Thanks so much, Ezra. I'll bring him back later. Here's ten more dollars for his board."

"He's welcome here anytime, Zack. Do you want a leg up? With one arm in a sling and that heavy thing on your back, I don't think you can swing up like you're used to."

Zack bent his leg, and Ezra boosted him up onto the horse. "See you later, Zack."

"Bye, Ezra, thanks."

It was a one minute ride from the livery to the saloon, but it was so good to be back on Echo's back, that Zack rode all around town. He loved the easy movement of the horse and the way Echo always answered when he talked to him. Looking down at his sore arm, Zack thought how lucky it was that it became infected. Otherwise he might never have known the pleasures of the twenty-first century, he might never have gotten Echo back, and he might never have had a chance to win Madison's heart. Not that it was exactly won yet, but he hoped it would be soon.

He slid off Echo's back and draped the reins over the hitching post. Zack knew he didn't need to tie the horse—Echo wasn't going anywhere. Looking over the top of the swinging doors into the saloon, Zack saw Matthew working at the bar and Sarah singing at the piano. This was the only home he'd known for the last four years, and he would miss it. But he knew he had to leave. Bringing beers and whiskeys to drunks and taking their insults, without saying a word, had grown old. He didn't need it anymore—not when he had the twenty-first century as an option.

Pushing open the swinging doors, he slowly walked in. Sarah saw him first. She left the piano and stopped singing in the middle of a song. "Zack! Zack! You're okay! I was so worried about you. I was afraid we'd never see you again!"

"Ouch! Not so tight, Sarah, my arm is still sore."

"Oh! Sorry, Zack."

When Matthew heard the commotion, he pushed between Sarah and Zack and made it a group hug. "We missed you, boy. Hope you're home to stay," said Matthew.

Zack smiled at the comment. Now was not the time to say anything—not with such a warm homecoming.

"We heard you'd be coming home today, so I cooked a special supper," said Matthew. "Rawlins is going to watch the bar, and we'll eat at a table—a regular family supper. It's so great to see you back and healthy again, Zack. Come on in. Can I bring your pack upstairs for you?"

"No, I can bring it upstairs. Thanks. When's supper?" Zack knew that Rawlins was the ex-drunk deputy sheriff, who still frequented the saloon, although he had stopped drinking after he assisted in rescuing Sarah.

"Whenever you're ready for it, Zack."

Zack considered asking if Madison could join them. But he thought with all the special treatment from Matthew and Sarah, he should just accept what it was. A family supper. And Madison wasn't family—yet. He hoped to have a chance to talk to Matthew about her. He needed some advice about women.

CHAPTER TWENTY-SEVEN

MATTHEW, SARAH, AND Zack sat down for supper. Matthew had prepared fried chicken, mashed potatoes, and spiced beets. It used to be Zack's favorite before he had tried Thai food, but Zack didn't say anything about that.

"So how was it in the future, Zack?" asked Matthew.

"It was awesome!"

"Awesome?" asked Sarah. "I think you were there too long! You're starting to talk like you're from the twenty-first century!"

"I can't figure out the attraction to such a place," said Matthew. "Why would anyone want to live there, when this is a choice?"

"I was perfectly happy there until I found the old Red Bluff. And you." Sarah looked at Matthew lovingly.

Matthew patted her hand. "That's what I mean. Once you've been here, why would you want to go anywhere else?"

"I believe that's what you said about Missouri before you left," laughed Sarah.

Matthew and Zack laughed with her. "Well, darling,

that much is true! I guess I'm not much of an explorer."

"So you thought it was awesome, huh, Zack? And how about Madison? How did you get along with her?"

"Madison is great," said Zack. He liked Sarah and trusted her, but he felt he needed a man's opinion about what to do with Madison. So he didn't want to mention his feelings with her around.

"What was in that backpack you brought back? It looked heavy," said Matthew.

"Mostly books. I went to a bookstore and bought a bunch of them."

"Twenty-first-century books, I imagine?" asked Sarah.

Zack nodded. "Madison loaned me *A Time to Kill* by John Grisham, and I bought the sequel."

"Oh, yes, you would like books about lawyers. Did you get any more Pennsylvania law books?" Sarah joked.

Zack smiled. "No, I don't think I need those anymore. I'm thinking of selling that one on eBay."

"eBay? What's eBay?" asked Matthew.

"eBay is an online marketplace. You can buy or sell almost anything there," Sarah said to Matthew. "Zack, does that mean you will return to the future, or will you ask Madison to sell it for you?"

Zack put another bite of chicken in his mouth before he answered. Although he wasn't looking at them, he knew that Sarah and Matthew were looking straight at him. He thought it was as good a time as any to tell them what he had planned. And he didn't have to mention Madison in his plans—not now anyway. "Yes, Sarah. I want to return. I want to live there—permanently."

Matthew, who was sipping his beer, choked on it. "Permanently? You're not serious!"

"Yes, Matthew, it's what I want. To move there and

not return."

"You can't do that, Zack! I need you here!" said Matthew.

"You have Sarah now, Matthew. You don't need me," said Zack quietly.

"Is that what you think? Is that why you're leaving? Because you think I don't want you around anymore? Because I do! You're family!" said Matthew.

Zack noticed that Sarah sat quietly and didn't say anything. He supposed that she thought it was between him and Matthew. And it was. "No, Matthew. That's not why I'm leaving. You're family to me, also. I'm leaving because there is opportunity there. What would I do here? Always be your side-pal? Serving drinks to men who call me names? Never getting anywhere in life? Dreaming my life away reading old books and never getting what I want out of life? Matthew, I don't want to hurt you. You have been wonderful to me. You *are* family. But you need to let me go, make my own life."

Matthew dabbed at his mouth, put the napkin down, and pushed his chair from the table. He glared at Sarah. "I can't take this. I can't believe it! I knew this would happen if you took him there."

"Would you rather I had left him here to die?" asked Sarah.

"No, of course not. It's just that I like things as they are. I don't like change."

"And I *need* a change, Matthew. I can't be serving drinks my whole life. It's different for you. You own the place. I want to be a lawyer—I've always wanted to be a lawyer. If I move to the new Red Bluff, I *can* be."

"You need to go to school to become a lawyer," said Matthew.

"I know that. I've already started preparing. That's what was in the backpack—books to help me get into college."

"Do you have a high school diploma?" asked Sarah.

"No. I'm going to take the GED test," said Zack.

"Zack's right, Matthew. He's a man. He needs to make his own way," said Sarah, patting Matthew's hand.

Matthew pulled his hand away. "I don't have to like it, do I?"

"No. You don't have to like it. But you have to love him enough that you can set him free without making him feel guilty about going," said Sarah.

"Why do you always know the exact right thing to say!" said Matthew, as he stood up and walked briskly out of the room.

Sarah looked at Zack, her eyes soft with concern. "Don't worry, Zack. When he gets used to the idea, he'll be fine. I'll help him through it. I think it's a great idea. Since I found out that you were reading a law book from Pennsylvania, I've been thinking that moving to the future would be a good opportunity for you. You go for it, Zack. Follow your heart."

CHAPTER TWENTY-EIGHT

GRANNY STEPPED TO the door and opened it. "C'mon. It's almost time for supper. You'll eat with us."

Not will you, or would you like to, just "you will." That was Granny all right. She was a dear old woman, but she could get annoying, thought Madison, as she stood up and followed Granny out the door.

"You're staying here tonight, right?" asked Granny. "I don't want you riding back in the dark. Maybe if you go through that cave in the dark, you'll end up in another time."

"Yes, I'm staying here. I was hoping to talk to you alone, though, Granny."

"We were just alone in my room. Whatever you have to talk about, you can talk about in front of the family. They're your family now, too, you know."

"I know, Granny, I know." Madison thought about asking if Zack could come to dinner, too, but he wasn't family—yet. Although she still needed to talk to Granny about him, she wasn't comfortable doing that in front of everyone else. A girl needs some privacy.

They walked down the stairs and into Eliza's dining

area. Madison had never been in there. It had a homey feeling, and the table was already set for five—like they expected her to be there.

"Go ahead, sit down, Madison," said Granny. Edward was just coming out of the kitchen carrying a platter of food. Granny grabbed him before he returned to the kitchen and wrapped her arms around him. Madison couldn't hear what she said to him, but then Edward said, "Madison! Don't make my woman cry, or you'll make me cry, too!" Then he kissed Granny on the forehead and walked back into the kitchen.

Madison sat at the table facing the window. Looking across the street, she saw a pinto horse at the hitching post close to the saloon. That must be Zack's horse, she thought. Zack. She needed to talk to Granny. Alone. Interrupting her thoughts, Eliza and her husband, Samuel, sat down, and then Granny and Edward sat down. Supper was a blur of easy conversation and good food. Madison wasn't sure if Edward or Samuel knew about the twenty-first century, so she didn't say anything about it. She did know, though, that Eliza had gone with Jenna once to see it.

All Madison could think about was Zack. She didn't even remember what she ate. When supper was over, Granny said, "All right, Madison, what did you want to talk about?"

Feeling awkward, Madison looked down and only said, "Ummmm."

Edward stood up abruptly. "Old woman! Don't you know any better than that? Young girls don't want to talk in front of men! Come on, Samuel. Let's exit the premises and let them talk girl-talk." Edward grabbed everyone's empty plates and headed for the kitchen.

Samuel smiled, picked up the rest of what was on the table, and followed Edward out.

"Are you sufficiently embarrassed now?" Granny asked Madison. "It's good for you. Now what's up?"

Madison looked from Granny to Eliza. She would have rather talked to Granny in private, but since Eliza had known Zack for years, maybe this would be even better. "It's Zack. I don't know what to do about Zack."

Granny balled up her fists. "Has that boy done something to you, Madison?"

Madison pushed Granny's fists away and smiled. "Only made me fall in love with him."

Granny put her hands on her hips. "Well, how dare he do that to my great-granddaughter!" Madison and Eliza laughed. "What are you going to do about it?" asked Granny.

"That's what I need to talk about. Zack doesn't even know how I feel."

"So I suppose you'll be wanting to move here, into the past, like the rest of the family," said Granny.

Madison perked up her head. "No. Definitely no. I'm a twenty-first-century girl. I don't mind coming occasionally to visit, but I don't want to live here. And I have no idea if Zack would want to leave here—or even if he feels the same way about me."

"I don't know how he feels about you, dear, but I can tell you this," said Eliza. "Leaving here would be the best thing that could happen for Zack. He's needed a kick in the pants to start doing something, and maybe this is it. He's been wasting away at that saloon. His only joy in life is his books. It would be a good opportunity for him to move to the future and get an education."

"Do you really think that's what he wants?" asked

Madison.

"I don't know whether or not he wants it," said Eliza. "But I know it would be good for him. And I don't think it would take much persuading to convince him of that. Zack has wanted to be a lawyer since Josiah first told him that he had gone to school in Boston to be one."

"Really?" asked Madison. "Josiah is a lawyer, too, like Aunt Jenna?"

"No, Josiah quit law school to move out here to the west. He wanted to be a lawman, not a lawyer."

"Oh. But what can I do about Zack? How can I find out if he feels the same way?"

"I'd go right up to that boy and say, 'So you want to sleep with me or not?' That's what I think you should do!" said Granny.

Eliza laughed. "I'm hoping she's kidding, Madison. I still don't know half the time! No, honey, I don't think you should say that to Zack. I think you should spend time with him and see what develops between you. He's never had a girlfriend, you know, so he might be a little shy. Give him time."

"That does sound like a great idea except for one huge obstacle. He lives more than a hundred years in the past. How can we spend time together if he's here and I'm there?"

"Like I said," said Granny. "Ask him straight out how he feels and then you'll know. Problem solved."

"The hundred years does complicate matters," said Eliza. "If you want to know immediately, then asking him might be the way to go. But if you want to go slow and give him time to act on his own, then just start coming here every weekend to visit your Granny. She wouldn't mind. You know you're welcome here anytime.

And that would give you the time you need to find out."

"If I were you, girl, I'd stop talking to us old fogies and get your young butt across the street to talk to him now. Time's a wastin'! Get going!" Granny stood up. "I'm going to go help the men. I'd go over there if I were you. Go for it!"

Eliza, always mothering, squeezed Madison's hands. "It will work out the way it's meant to, Madison. Go on over and talk to him. Enjoy your time with him. Maybe the evening will unfold exactly how you would like it to."

CHAPTER TWENTY-NINE

AFTER ZACK HELPED Sarah clean up, he walked straight outside without looking at Matthew who was behind the bar. Zack stroked Echo's face and said, "There's my good boy, Echo. Just being around you makes me feel better. How did I get along without you for so long? We'll never be apart again, Echo. I promise." Then he whispered in the horse's ear, "I hope you like living in the twenty-first century, 'cause that's where we're going!"

He took the reins and led the horse into the street. With only one good arm, he couldn't swing up on the horse. Although he had enough "old" money to buy a saddle, he didn't think it would be that long before he could swing up again. Kat had not yet given him permission to take the sling off, but he thought it would be soon. Zack led the horse the long way around to the livery, stroking him the whole way. And with every word that Zack spoke to him, Echo nickered in reply.

After putting the horse back in his stall, Zack reluctantly walked back to the saloon. Matthew didn't want to talk to him at all. What was Zack going to do? He pushed open the swinging doors, strode inside and up the stairs to his room. He chose the new book by John Grisham and walked back downstairs to his usual table. Sarah was singing, Matthew was at the bar, and Zack was reading. Everything seemed back to normal except that Matthew was angry, and Zack was in love and planning to leave the old Red Bluff.

When Sarah finished her song, she walked over to the bar and said something to Matthew. Without looking up, Matthew nodded his head and put down the glass he was washing. Sarah returned to the piano, and Matthew walked over to Zack. Although Zack had watched the entire interaction, he pretended he was reading when Matthew sat down on the opposite side of the table.

"Sarah said I need to talk to you," said Matthew glumly.

Zack nodded his head but didn't say a word.

"I guess I should say I'm sorry for acting that way. I *am* sorry. But you're like a little brother to me, Zack, and I'll miss you so much!"

"You'll still see me, Matthew. It's not like I'm never coming back. I'm less than an hour away. You know that. I know you've been there."

"But I'm used to having you here every day. It won't be the same. Like I said, I don't like change."

"Sarah was a big change, and you liked that change."

"Sarah was an addition to my life. If you leave—well, when you leave—it will be a subtraction."

"I'm sorry, Matthew. I have to do it. There is no way for me to be a lawyer in the nineteenth century. But there *is* a way in the twenty-first. I wouldn't be true to myself if I stayed here and just dreamed about something that is within my grasp."

"You're right, Zack. I know you are. It will just take

me some time to get used to you being gone. I'll be okay," said Matthew, as he smiled a sad smile at Zack.

"Can I talk to you about something else?" Zack fidgeted in his seat.

"Sure, Zack, anything. I really apologize for how I acted. What do you want to talk about?"

"Madison."

"Madison? Is she the reason you want to move to the new Red Bluff?" Matthew asked, raising his voice.

"No. The main reason is that I want to be a lawyer. I want to make something of myself. But if I could be with Madison, too, then it would make everything that much more awesome."

"Awesome." Matthew shook his head. "You already talk like you belong there."

"So what should I do?"

"About what?"

"Madison! What should I do about Madison?"

"What do you mean?"

"Matthew, I don't know if she likes me or not. And I don't know how to find out or tell her that I like her."

"Oh. Oh." Matthew exhaled slowly. "Why don't you ask her out for supper? That would be a good start."

"You mean at the hotel?" Zack moved his head to indicate the hotel across the street from the saloon.

"No, Zack, I mean in the new Red Bluff. There's a Thai restaurant there that has delicious food. Sarah took me there."

"We ate there a few days ago. It was delicious."

"So invite her back there. Or someplace else. I know there's more than one restaurant there."

"Okay," said Zack slowly. "That is a good idea. But maybe she'd think it was to repay her for staying at her house for a week."

"I don't know, Zack! Then just kiss her! If she kisses you back, then she likes you, too. If she slaps your face, then she doesn't. Although that's not always true, either. When Edward first kissed Granny, at her birthday party, she slapped him and then kissed him back. I don't know, Zack. I guess the best advice would be to go with the moment. If it feels like you should ask her for supper, then ask. If it feels like you should kiss her, then kiss. All I can say is good luck. I have to get back to the bar now. I love ya, kid."

"Thanks, Matthew. I appreciate your help."

CHAPTER THIRTY

As Madison opened the door of the hotel and stepped outside, she saw that Zack's horse wasn't in front of the saloon anymore. She wondered if he had returned the horse to the livery and if he was back yet. She looked at the saloon, the horses tied in front, and the dirt street, and she thought about what a different life it would have been growing up in this environment. How could someone who grew up like this, and she, who grew up in the twenty-first century, have anything in common? How could they form a life together? Could they overcome the differences? But Zack fit in so well in the twenty-first century. It really was like he belonged there. She wondered if he thought so.

Madison crossed the street, pushed through the swinging doors of the saloon, and saw Zack sitting at the back table reading a book. Sarah had just finished singing a song, so Madison walked up to her. "Hey, Sarah, how's it going?"

"Hi, Madison! Thank you for bringing Zack back."

Madison noticed that Zack had picked up his head, seemingly at the sound of her voice. He smiled at her, and she returned the smile. "Oh, you're welcome, Sarah. Talk to you later." She walked over to Zack's table and sat down.

"Hi, stranger," said Madison.

Zack laughed. "It does seem like we've been apart for ages, although it's only been a few hours." When he looked at her, his eyes twinkled. Did they always do that?

"I saw your horse outside before. He is beautiful. I bet it feels good to have him back."

Zack slowly shook his head back and forth. "I never thought he'd be mine again. It's like a miracle. Really, Madison, a miracle. Thank you."

"I didn't do anything," said Madison.

"You told me about the coins! And that's what allowed me to get him back."

"I'm just glad you have him again. I know what it's like to love your horse."

"Hey, chief! Get over here and gimme some whiskey!" called a voice from the poker table at the other side of the room.

"I'll be right back, Madison," said Zack, as he stood up, grabbed a bottle from the bar, and took it over to the poker table.

When he returned, Madison asked, "Why do they call you chief? Is that your nickname or something?"

Zack frowned. "I wouldn't exactly call it a nickname. They call me that because my mother was Indian." He looked at Madison, almost defiantly, through half closed eyes. "I'm half Indian. Does that bother you?"

"Bother me? That you're half Indian, as you call it?" Madison laughed.

"Why are you laughing?"

"Because I'm half Indian, too! Only they call it Native

American in the twenty-first century."

"You're half Indian? Really? No, you're trying to hornswoggle me!"

Madison held her right hand up. "Honest Injun, Zack! I'm half Native American!" She laughed again and shook her head. "I thought you knew. You've seen my last name, haven't you?"

"No," said Zack. "What does that have to do with anything?"

"My last name is Two Feathers," said Madsion.

Zack smiled at her again, and the twinkle returned to his eyes. "I can't believe it. Something else that we have in common. We both want to be lawyers, and we're both half Indian, er, Native American. It's going to take me awhile to get that one straight."

"That's okay, but you might offend some people in the meantime. Although, since you *are* Native American, too, it shouldn't bother them too much."

"Chief! Another round here! Now!" screamed someone from across the room.

Zack grimaced and stood up, but Rawlins appeared from the back and pushed him back down. "I'll take care of it, kid. You talk to your friend."

"Thanks, Rawlins."

As Zack sat down, Madison said, "Don't you ever think about standing up to them?"

"No," said Zack. "Never. Sarah stood up for me. She walked over there and poured whiskey in the guy's lap when he wouldn't stop calling me chief."

"Wow, that was cool of Sarah to do that."

"And she ended up getting kidnapped by the guy."

"That was just one guy. Not all jerks are kidnappers."

"There's something else," said Zack. "There's another

reason that I'll just take it and not say anything. My father got shot standing up for himself. In this saloon—just before Matthew and Josiah moved to town."

"Oh, Zack, I'm sorry. I understand now."

"It's been nearly four years."

"Chief! More whiskey!"

"I just brought you whiskey," said Rawlins.

"It tastes better when the chief pours it," said the man.

Matthew walked up to their table and looked at Zack. "Why don't you take Madison for a walk outside so this scalawag will forget about you? I think that's easier than throwing him out."

Zack stood up and handed Matthew his book to set behind the bar. Then he put out his hand to help Madison stand, and they walked out of the saloon together.

CHAPTER THIRTY-ONE

MADISON COULDN'T BELIEVE it. The one part of her identity that she had always felt strongest about was her Native American heritage. And now she finds out the man she has fallen in love with is also Native American. She wanted to scream out to the world how happy she was, but she stayed silent as she walked out the swinging doors beside Zack.

"Do you mind walking around town?" asked Zack.

"No, not at all," said Madison.

They walked in silence until they reached the end of the street. Zack turned left, past the Ralston General Store, and said, "Um, Madison, there's something I've been wanting to talk to you about."

Surely this was the moment that he would say how he felt. Madison felt the joy building inside her. She wasn't sure she could contain it. Instead, as calmly as she could, she said, "Sure, Zack. I'm listening."

"I've been thinking about this a lot, and I, um—"

When he hesitated, she said, "Yes," to encourage him. She smiled at him, but he was looking at the ground instead of at her.

"Um, I want to move to the future. I want to go to school there and become a lawyer."

Madison tried to conceal her disappointment, but she feared that her shaky voice gave her away. "Ah, I told you, Zack, that I thought you'd make a terrific lawyer."

"Do you really think so?" asked Zack, smiling at her and obviously not noticing the quiver in her voice. That annoyed Madison. But he was probably nervous about confessing this to her and more focused on himself.

Madison exhaled. "Yes, yes, I do. You'll have a lot of school in front of you, though. Four years of college before you even get into law school. And you'll have to take that GED test that we talked about."

"I already bought the books and study guides for the test," said Zack.

"You did? Wow, I didn't know that. You *are* serious." Madison chastised herself for being upset at his disclosure. She wanted him to live in the twenty-first century. Now he confirms it, and she's disappointed that he didn't declare his undying love to her. Give him time, she told herself. One confession at a time. Encourage his choice and be supportive. "I'll help you in any way I can, Zack."

"That would be awesome, Madison. I still don't know exactly what I need to do after I pass the GED."

"You need to apply to college. Sooner would be better than later, if you want a chance to get in this fall. You'll also need to take either the SAT or the ACT. When is the GED?"

"The guy at the bookstore asked me that and scared me. So I looked it up, and apparently this year they've changed it. It's computerized, and you can take the test almost any time. I figure I'll be ready in a week. Do you think that will give me enough time to apply for college?"

"A week! It's a long test, from what I understand. Several parts to it and all. And most of the information —has happened in the past one hundred years. How are you going to learn all that in one week?"

Zack smiled at her. "I'm a fast learner, Madison."

"Oh, that's right. You have a photographic memory! Well, that will definitely be an asset. There is one thing, though."

"What?"

"College is expensive."

"I have a plan for that. I'm not sure it's going to work, but I'll start on that after I get through the GED test."

"What's your plan? I hope you're not planning to rob the bank or anything!"

Zack laughed. "No, nothing like that. But I did buy a coin book at the bookstore. I know what coins are valuable and how to determine which coins are worth more. I'm hoping it won't be difficult to find the more valuable ones. And I'll be on the lookout for the 1795 silver dollar the coin guy wants. That would be a ton of money right there." They had circled the block and arrived back in front of the saloon again. Zack stopped in front of the saloon and said, "I don't want to take you back in there and expose you to that nonsense. Do you want to go into the hotel and talk?"

Madison, without a moment's hesitation, said, "No, Zack. I think I'm ready to go in for the night. It was nice talking to you. I'll probably see you in the morning before I ride home."

"Come on. I'll walk you over there." They walked across the street. Zack stepped in front of Madison so he could open the hotel door for her. But before he opened it, he leaned over and kissed Madison on the lips. "I like you, Madison."

She leaned into him, and when he pulled away, she kissed him back. "I like you, too, Zack." Then she stepped through the door and ran up the stairs to her room.

CHAPTER THIRTY-TWO

MADISON COULDN'T SLEEP. She lay in bed thinking that she had acted like a first grader, after all. "I like you, too, Zack!" she had said. At least she had kissed him back, although it wasn't much of a kiss. But it was enough for a first kiss, she thought. Well, now she knew he had feelings for her, and she knew that he wanted to move to the twenty-first century. Where did that leave them? On the road to happiness or disaster? The real question was whether a man from the nineteenth century could find lasting happiness in the twenty-first century.

She knew that her Aunt Jenna, Sarah, and even her Uncle Ryan had successfully moved *from* the twenty-first century back to the nineteenth. They had all adjusted well and were happy—although they did make occasional trips to the future for various reasons. But could someone from the past be happy in the future? Zack was young enough to adjust. And it would be great for him to get away from those awful men who called him names. He did want to go to college and become a lawyer. It seemed like the future was a good fit for him. And he could return to the past any time he wanted to. With the cave, it didn't have to be an either/or choice.

Zack had already bought books to study for the GED test! He was serious about going to college. Was becoming a lawyer more important to him than she was? It was still early to be wondering about that. Maybe he just wanted to use her so he could go to school. Madison chided herself for thinking that about Zack. The one thing she felt certain of: there was nothing at all deceitful about Zack. What you saw was what you got. The men in her time were complicated, manipulating, and looking out for their own good. That's what she liked about Zack. He was innocent of all those confusing behaviors. He was just—Zack.

She closed her eyes again hoping to get some sleep. Five minutes later, she opened them. Too many thoughts —about Zack—swirled around in her mind. Madison reached for her backpack and fished out her iPhone. Midnight. How long had she been lying there unable to sleep? Too long. She touched the screen and all her music appeared. Moving her finger on the screen, she selected some soft music that she hoped would lull her to sleep.

It worked. Madison didn't wake until morning when she heard Granny pounding on her door and shouting, "Up and at 'em, great-granddaughter. You can't be sleeping the day away! It's time for breakfast! Come on! Get up!"

That was enough to rouse the dead, thought Madison. She stretched, dressed, and walked downstairs. No one was in the hotel lobby, so she went to the door that led to Eliza and Samuel's private quarters. Private, except they always kept the door open. She peeked in, and although no one was seated at the table, it was again set for five.

Like they were expecting her. Like she really *was* family. Madison liked the feeling.

A minute later, four people came bustling out of the kitchen carrying plates stacked with french toast, preserves, and a coffee pot. Everyone said hello to Madison, set down everything they were holding, sat down, and started eating.

"Glad to see you made it to breakfast, Madison. I thought you would sleep all day!" said Granny.

"Granny, it's only eight o'clock."

"We get up early in the nineteenth century! And I like it that way!" said Granny.

Everyone else mumbled their agreement and kept eating. When breakfast was over, Madison was grateful that neither Eliza nor Granny had brought up Zack or asked what had happened with him. And wanting to keep it that way, Madison helped carry the dishes into the kitchen, and then said her good-byes. She needed to say good-bye to Zack, though, so instead of going to her room, she walked across the street to the saloon.

The main door to the saloon was still closed, because they weren't open this early in the morning. Madison knocked on the door. A few seconds later, Zack opened the door with a big smile on his face.

"I knew it would be you!"

"Hi, Zack! I just wanted to say good-bye before I left to go home."

"You're leaving so early? I thought we could spend some time together before you left."

"I need to get back," said Madison, gauging his response.

"Oh, okay," said Zack, his smile fading.

"So, I'll see you in town when you come to take your

test, right? About a week?"

"Yeah, next Sunday is what I was thinking."

"You know you're welcome any time, Zack. Just come on in! You can't let me know, anyway."

"Okay," said Zack.

Madison looked around. It was morning, but although there was no one on the street, it didn't feel appropriate to kiss him out in the open like this. "Okay, bye." Madison started walking toward the livery stable, then turned around. "Oh, I forgot my stuff! Anyway, bye, Zack. I'm looking forward to seeing you next Sunday."

"Bye, Madison," said Zack.

Madison rushed up the steps of the hotel to the second floor where her room was. She packed, straightened the room, talked to Eliza for a few minutes at the front desk, and stepped outside to a surprise.

Zack was there in front of the hotel, bareback on his horse, and holding the reins on Chaco and Paisley, who were already saddled. "Hi, Madison. I thought I'd get the horses for you. And ride a ways with you—if you don't mind."

Madison's grin spread across her whole face. "Zack! Of course I don't mind. This was so sweet of you! But I owe you for the board on the horses."

"No, Madison. I stayed at your house for a week. It's the least I can do."

Madison hooked her backpack onto Paisley's saddle, pulled the reins over Chaco's head, and climbed up. "Let's go!"

CHAPTER THIRTY-THREE

ZACK FELT SO relieved when he saw Madison's wide smile. He hadn't been sure if he had done the right thing by getting the horses and offering to ride back with her. There was a chance, he thought, that she was just trying to get away from him. So when he saw her smile, his whole body relaxed.

"Have you—" said Madison.

"I started—" said Zack.

"Sorry," they said in unison.

"Go ahead," said Madison.

"I started studying for the GED last night and studied more this morning. I'm sure I can do it."

"I know you can, Zack! When did you say the test was again?"

"Oh, when I looked it up, I thought you could take it anytime."

"There are probably certain times, and you have to sign up for when you want to take it."

"I didn't realize that. When I discovered it wasn't just a few times a year, I stopped reading about it."

"It might be once or twice a week, or maybe once or

twice a month. And I'm sure you have to sign up for it."

"So if I come Sunday and want to take it Monday, that probably won't work, huh?"

"I doubt if it works that quickly." They turned off to the side trail, with Madison in the lead, Paisley following, and Zack at the rear. "See the cow pies pushed under the bushes? That's what the rustler did to hide the tracks of the cows that he stole. And here's the cave."

"I'll ride with you a little farther."

They entered the cave, and their conversation stopped. "Oh, look, here is the fence panel the rustler used to block the other entrance when he brought the cattle through here!"

"Why didn't we see it before?"

"He hid it in a good place. You either have to know where it is in the shadows, or have the light from the crack above exactly right."

They exited the cave, and Madison stopped her horse to let Zack catch up. "I should go back now, Madison. I don't want to ride all the way."

"Listen, Zack, if you want, I can sign you up and schedule a test for next week."

"That would be awesome! You wouldn't mind?"

"Not at all. I'd be happy to do it."

"Thanks, Madison." Zack leaned over and kissed Madison. "Then I'll see you Sunday!"

"I'm looking forward to it, Zack!" Madison leaned over and kissed him back. "Bye!"

Zack didn't move his horse. He watched as Madison and the two horses turned in front of the bush that hid the cave. As he was about to go back into the cave, he saw Madison's horse appear again.

"Zack! I'm glad you didn't go back yet. I need more

information about you so I can sign you up."

"Sure, what?"

"Your full name and your birthday. I know they'll ask for that."

"Zackary Allen Murphy. April 14, 1848."

"Oh, dear. That will never do. This may be more difficult than we had anticipated. Your new birthday will be . . . April 14, 1992. And I can use my address and the house phone number for you. We'll get it done, Zack. Don't worry. Oh, wait, spell your name for me."

"Z-a-c-k-a-r-y A-l-l-e-n M-u-r-p-h-y."

"Okay! Bye again!"

"Bye, Madison. Thank you so much!" Again he watched as she headed toward the bush. This time, she turned around, gave him a warm smile that sent his stomach into somersaults, and then disappeared down the trail.

Although he could no longer see her, he could still hear the two horses walking down the trail. When the sound of horse hooves faded, and all he could hear were birds and the sound of the wind through the trees, Zack smiled to himself and sighed as he turned his horse back toward the cave. He loved that girl. He was completely smitten, and it felt wonderful. She had kissed him back again. There was no mistaking it. She felt the same about him. He was going to be a lawyer, and he was going to be with the girl of his dreams. Life couldn't get any sweeter.

CHAPTER THIRTY-FOUR

EVEN AFTER MADISON had turned the corner and knew that Zack couldn't see her anymore, she felt his eyes on her. It was like he was still there, with her. A feeling of warmth ran through her. Oh, she did like that boy! Although she had just left him, she could hardly wait to see him again.

It was still morning, but the sound of the horses' hooves on the hard-packed trail and romantic thoughts about Zack lulled her into a peaceful, almost sleepy feeling. He was going to take the GED! That brought him one step closer to moving to the twenty-first century *and* to her.

Madison breathed in the scents of the pines and listened to the wind gently blowing through the trees. Soon, the back corral came into view. She walked the horses through the two gates, put them in their respective stalls, and walked dreamily into the house with a smile on her face. It felt like her feet weren't even touching the ground.

Immediately, she opened her laptop and googled, "GED test registration." When she clicked on the website where she thought Zack had found his information, she realized the first thing that Zack needed was an email account. After a quick visit to gmail to set up an account for Zack—using her name as the password, of course—she returned to the online GED site and signed him up.

Everything went smoothly until she came to the section that asked about the highest grade completed in school. What should she put for that? Reading over the possible answers, she chose, "I don't remember the highest grade I completed." Madison thought that would be the safest. The next tough question was, "In what year was the last year of schooling completed?" 1865-ish. That would never do! She'd have to ad-lib on that one! She continued to ad-lib more of the answers—work status, income, where did you study for the GED—the questions went on and on.

When she arrived at the page asking for a social security number, she felt relieved when it said "optional." If she hadn't been so hasty with her relief, she might have anticipated the problems yet to occur. Madison also neglected clicking the "testing policies" link. If she had, she would have discovered something unsettling. But as it was, she scheduled the "Reasoning through Language Arts" test for the following Tuesday, then closed her computer and called her mother.

"Hey, Mom."

"Hi, Madison. Did you get Zack settled back into the past?"

"Yes, he's back at the saloon now, safe, and feeling much better than when he left! Thank you!"

"Did he take off the sling?"

"You never told him to, Mom."

"Damn. I meant to and must have forgotten. He

doesn't really need it now—it's healed so quickly. Although he shouldn't be lifting anything heavy for a while longer."

"Mom, you ragged on Doctor Mercer so much, and here you've made a mistake, too. Granted, it's not a critical mistake, but he can only work with what he knows. And back then, doctors didn't know much."

"You sound like you're defending him, Madison. I didn't even realize you'd met him."

"I haven't. Just sayin'."

"Okay, point made. Maybe I need to give him a textbook on Louis Pasteur and basic hygiene."

"Might not be a bad idea," said Madison. "But then he'd know where you're from. I mean when."

"Practically half the town is from my 'when'! My own brother and sister live there now, for heaven's sake! What's this world coming to? Next, you'll be telling me that you're moving back there." Kat hesitated and then continued, "You're not, are you, Madison? You're not planning to move back there, are you?"

"No, Mom. I'm definitely not moving back there! No worries!"

"Oh, good, because I thought maybe— Well, I'm glad you're not. I don't know what I'd do if I was the only one left of the family to live here! I may not always show it, Madison, but I like having you around. You're important to me."

"Thanks, Mom. I need to run now," said Madison, uncomfortable with her mother's admission.

"Okay, Mad. I'll talk to you later. Love you."

"Love you, too, Mom. Bye."

CHAPTER THIRTY-FIVE

As Zack and Echo walked slowly through the cave, he noticed the fence panel again. He leaned down to feel it and tried to pick it up with his good arm. It surprised him how heavy it felt. Letting go, he continued through the cave into the bright sunshine on the other side. Closing his eyes, he inhaled the fresh aroma of his surroundings. Would he miss it here? Was he not giving enough credit to the value of living here—here in the nineteenth century? He would proceed with his plan to take the GED test, but he'd have to give it some thought. Maybe he was being too hasty in his decision to get out of the old Red Bluff—to leave everything that he knew behind.

Continuing at a slow pace, Zack and the horse approached town. He wasn't in any hurry to get there; he just wanted to enjoy the feeling of being on Echo's back again. But the dark thoughts of missing the old Red Bluff started to intrude on his happy thoughts of moving to the new Red Bluff. The new Red Bluff held everything he had ever wanted—being a lawyer and loving a good woman. And the old Red Bluff held everything that he had known and had once held dear.

When Zack had first decided to leave, he hadn't expected the internal struggle that he was now experiencing. Would it go away? Zack didn't know the answer to that, but he did know that he had to go forward with taking the GED test. If he had to acknowledge the corn, then maybe feeling unsure about passing the test made him insecure about the whole move. Study. He just had to study. That was the solution to that part of the problem, anyway.

Zack walked Echo into his stall, took off his bridle, and gave him a good brush down. Then he hugged him and walked to the saloon. As he walked inside, he looked around the room and realized that so much of his life in Red Bluff was his life in this saloon. He knew almost everyone. Matthew was like a brother to him.

When he heard Sarah tinkering with something in the back room, he smiled. Life was comfortable here. Not satisfying, but comfortable. Was he willing to give up a life that was comfortable and familiar for a life that was full of the unknown? Zack had security here. But in the twenty-first century, he had opportunity and possibility. And it wasn't like once he left he couldn't come back. Yet a part of him didn't want to leave. That part clung to the familiar and the security of what he had always known.

"Zack? You okay?" As Sarah bustled out of the kitchen, she saw him still standing and dreaming at the entrance to the saloon.

"Oh, yeah, Sarah, fine, thank you." Zack walked through the saloon to the stairs and jumped them two at a time all the way to the top. Stepping into his room, he gathered up his GED books. Which one should I start with, he wondered. Leafing through them, he picked up the one with sample questions.

Turning to the history section, Zack found this question:

Mussolini ruled Italy from 1922 to 1943. His type of government was called:
A. Democracy
B. Oligarchy
C. Monarchy
D. Communism
E. Dictatorship

1922. That was more than fifty years in Zack's future. Perhaps he should start with something easier and work up to history. Choosing the book on language arts, he put the rest back in the drawer and returned downstairs, sitting at his usual table in the back by the bar. He had just opened the book when Sarah sat down across from him with a sly smile on her face.

"Did you ride with Madison back to Red Bluff?"

"No, not all the way," said Zack hesitantly.

"Did you kiss her?"

Zack frowned, his hands involuntarily squeezed into fists, and he glanced at Matthew who was pouring a beer for someone at the bar. Sarah leaned across the table and patted one of Zack's fists.

"Oh, Zack, don't be mad at him. I forced it out of him. He honestly didn't tell me voluntarily."

Zack's fists relaxed, but he looked at Sarah with narrowed eyes. "That conversation should stay between us men."

Sarah put her head down. "I'm sorry, Zack. You're right. It's none of my business. But I was excited that my matchmaking efforts paid off."

"Matchmaking? What do you mean?"

"Do you remember the first time you met Madison? Eliza and Samuel were having a birthday party for Granny at their hotel?"

"Yes, and I was watching the saloon, while Matthew was at the party. Madison came over to give me a message."

"Who do you think sent her over here to give you the message?" Sarah cocked her head at him and smiled.

"You did?" Zack relaxed as a smile spread across his face.

Sarah nodded and stood up to leave. "Mission accomplished," she said, as she tapped Zack on the shoulder and walked away.

Zack smiled to himself and picked up the book that was in front of him. Opening it to the table of contents, he started reading but couldn't focus on the words. All he saw was Madison's face in front of him—the way she was that first time he saw her—when Sarah had sent her into the saloon.

He remembered looking up as someone came through the swinging doors. Madison. His heart leaped that first time he had seen her. She had just come to deliver a message, but they talked until the party across the street had ended. At that time, he didn't know if he'd ever see her again, but now, thinking back on that night, that moment, he realized that was when he started loving Madison. She had captured his heart the moment she walked through the door.

Thank you, Sarah, Zack said to himself.

CHAPTER THIRTY-SIX

LATER THAT AFTERNOON, when Zack's head had cleared and he could read again without thoughts of Madison intruding, he managed to get through half the book. Studying carefully and taking the sample test at the end of each chapter, he felt good about his progress. He had only missed one question after reading eight chapters; and when he missed that one, he read the chapter again. So he felt good about himself, and fortunately, he had been left alone because Rawlins was helping Matthew.

He had just started a new chapter, when suddenly a hand appeared in front of him and swept the book onto the floor. At the same time Zack heard raucous laughter, the man's foot stomped on the book bending its pages.

"How's that, chief? You shouldn't be reading when I need whiskey!"

Before the man could turn away, Zack had stood up, and with his good arm, he had planted a sockdologer on the man's face so hard that the man hit the floor. Zack bent over, and with his foot, pushed the man's arm away and picked up his book. Without looking around, he marched upstairs to his room without a second thought.

He was not going to put up with garbage like that anymore.

Walking into his room, he propped himself on the bed and kept reading. It didn't occur to him until he came to the end of the chapter that perhaps Matthew might be angry that Zack had punched one of his customers. The man had deserved it. Zack wasn't going to be sorry. But if Matthew was angry, then Zack would apologize to him. There were enough hurt feelings going around as it was. Zack didn't want to leave town with Matthew in a huff.

Before he had a chance to begin reading the next chapter, someone knocked on the door. Zack swung his legs over the bed so he was sitting up. "Come in."

Matthew and Sarah strode in carrying three glasses and a bottle. Zack didn't have to wonder if Matthew was angry—there was a huge smile on his face. Sarah held up one glass of the sparkly liquid. "To the winner and still champion!"

Matthew handed Zack a glass and said, "I know you don't like to drink, Zack, but this deserves a glass of champagne! It took you long enough!"

Zack, confused, said, "You're not mad?"

"Mad? Why should I be mad? You should have done that long ago—and it probably would have been the last time you had to do it. I don't think anyone will bother you anymore, Zack! Now maybe you can decide to stay here instead of leaving." Although Matthew still held up his glass in a toasting position, the smile had faded from his face.

Zack put down his glass of champagne and gave Matthew a big hug, spilling Matthew's champagne all over both of them. "I'm sorry, Matthew. I have to leave.

But you're awesome. You're the best brother anybody could ever have."

Matthew patted Zack's back and pulled away. "It's okay, Zack. I understand. I really do."

Zack nodded, picked up his glass of champagne, and clinked glasses with Matthew and Sarah. He took a sip and handed the glass back to Matthew. "I can't have any more right now, Matthew. I'm in the middle of studying for my test. *That's* what made me so mad. That guy smashed my *book*." Zack picked up his book and showed Matthew and Sarah the bent pages. "It's *my* book. No one has the right to do that. It's one thing to call me chief, but it's another altogether to hurt my book." Then he held the book to his chest.

Matthew and Sarah nodded, and Sarah encouraged Matthew toward the door. "We understand, Zack. Now we'll leave you to your studying. C'mon, Matthew."

After they left the room, Zack realized that Sarah had not mentioned that both he and Matthew had tears in their eyes from the interaction. Maybe Josiah was right. Tears just showed that Zack and Matthew both had heart. And it hadn't bothered Sarah at all. He wondered if it would bother Madison.

CHAPTER THIRTY-SEVEN

MADISON WAS COUNTING the days until Zack came back to the twenty-first century, but she had the feeling that counting just made the time go slower. She wanted to see him so much, maybe too much. She'd have to think about that one.

By the end of the day Wednesday, she had decided that as much as she wanted to see Zack, she shouldn't be alone with him until after his GED test. She could probably get a friend to spend the night one night, but probably not two. How could she get a message to Zack not to come until Monday—the day before his test?

Madison glanced at the clock. Four thirty. A half hour more. It had been a busy day, and she was eager to return home. Too bad there wasn't a legitimate way to get out of the last half hour of work. As she turned back to her computer, Marcus strode through the door, carrying more dry cleaning. She looked at him questioningly.

"Madison. I would like for you to take my clothes to the dry cleaners and pick them up in the morning. Just tell them they're mine, and they'll know how to handle them." He stopped and held his hand up, palm out.

"Now before you say no, I want to say that I know you're not on salary, so you can go ahead and leave *now*. That should give you plenty of time to drop it off. And come in a half hour later tomorrow. Is that fair?"

"More than fair, Marcus. It won't take me longer than fifteen extra minutes."

"That's okay, Madison. Go ahead and take the half hour, now and in the morning. Be sure to tell them they are mine. The last person used her own name and ordered extra starch. I *hate* extra starch. I'm counting on you to take care of this."

Madison bit her lip to keep from laughing. "Yes, Marcus. I'm sure I can handle that. No problem."

He handed her the clothes and rushed out of the room. Madison powered down her computer with a smile on her face. Ask and it shall be given. She wanted a way out of the last half hour of work, and she got it! Life was sweet.

She gathered her belongings, left the office, and stepped into her car. Five minutes later, she had arrived at the dry cleaners, given them the clothes and Marcus's name, and was back in her car. Several minutes after that, she was home. Jenna's truck had been moved. That was curious, thought Madison. Jenna and Josiah normally only came once a month. When she opened the door, the two dogs greeted her. And as she walked into the living room, there was Josiah in his usual spot: feet propped up on the coffee table and holding the remote.

"'Good afternoon, Josiah. Surprised to see you here today," said Madison.

"Jenna needed something in town. Couldn't do without it. You know how women are. Oh! Sorry, Madison!" He turned back to the television.

As Madison walked to her room and passed Jenna's bedroom, she had an idea. She knocked on Jenna's door and stepped in. "Hi, Jenna."

"Hi, Madison. Bet you're surprised to see us here today," said Jenna.

"Yes, I am. Listen, Jenna, any chance you have some time to talk? Girl-talk?" asked Madison.

"Sure, Madison. Come on in," said Jenna, as she turned her chair around and motioned for Madison to sit on the end of the bed. "What is it, girlfriend?" Jenna was officially her aunt—her mother's sister—but they were so close to the same age they were more like friends.

"It's Zack. I don't want him to come Sunday night as he's planned. I don't want to be alone with him."

Jenna looked concerned. "You're not afraid of Zack, are you, Madison? Because he really likes you. I don't think he'd do anything to hurt you."

"No, Jenna. I'm not afraid of Zack. I'm afraid of myself. I don't want to be alone with him until after he takes his GED test. I want him to have his whole concentration on the test. I don't want him to be thinking of other things. You know." Madison raised her eyebrows at Jenna.

Jenna, studying her fingernails as Madison talked, started to say, "No, what do you—" Then she looked at Madison and understood. "Oh! You mean—oh! Okay! But what do you want me to do?"

"If you could ask him not to come until Monday night, it would be awesome. And if you and Josiah could come back Monday night, it would even be awesome-er! Although Josiah probably wouldn't want to come back so soon, but if you could just tell Zack, I'd appreciate it."

"What? Did that ole boy tell you it was my idea to

he loved.

CHAPTER THIRTY-NINE

MONDAY MORNING, ZACK awoke early and packed everything he was taking with him, which consisted of his books, pajamas, and clean underwear. Then he walked downstairs, had breakfast with Matthew and Sarah, and parked himself at his normal seat at the edge of the bar. After an hour of wondering how soon Jenna and Josiah would come get him, he decided to take off his sling. When he returned to this century, his arm should be healed enough to help Matthew again—for the short duration of time that he figured he'd stay at the old Red Bluff.

Sarah came and sat down in the seat opposite him. "You're excited, aren't you?"

"Oh, Sarah. I can't wait! This is the beginning of my new life. If this all works out, I'll be at college in the fall."

Sarah reached out and squeezed his hand. "You'll do great, Zack. You'll make a great lawyer. Do you think, though, that Jenna and Josiah will leave this early? Don't they usually leave later in the afternoon?"

"Yes, but they must know how excited I am to be going. I thought maybe they'd adjust."

"Maybe they will," said Sarah, smiling. "Maybe they will." She gave his hand another squeeze and walked away.

Sarah was so sweet, thought Zack. She and Matthew were so perfect for each other. Zack wondered if he and Madison were perfect for each other. He thought so.

The hours dragged on. After sitting there for some time fidgeting, he finally dragged out the book he had bought on test-taking strategies, and he began reading it. It was difficult to keep his mind on the book when every time the wind jostled the front doors, his head sprang up to see if it was Jenna or Josiah walking in. So far, it wasn't.

Dinnertime came, and he shared dinner in the back room, prepared by Sarah. She finally got angry when he kept jumping up from the table to see if someone had come through the door. "You'll know when they come, Zack. I guarantee they won't leave without you. Guaranteed! And if they do, you know the way yourself."

"Okay, sorry, Sarah."

When he heard another sound and involuntarily jumped, Sarah said, "Oh, Zack! I'm sorry. I understand. Finish your lunch and go back out there. You'll feel more comfortable waiting out there."

"Thanks, Sarah." He stuffed the last bite in his mouth and hugged Sarah. Then he squeezed Matthew's shoulders and skipped out to the main room of the saloon to wait.

It was getting later and later, and still Josiah and Jenna hadn't come for him. Maybe, he thought, he was supposed to go to them. Leaving his backpack in the seat and his book on the table, he walked down toward Josiah's office. Looking through the window, he saw

Josiah talking to two ranchers. Jenna was nowhere around. Apparently they weren't waiting for him. Josiah was still working on sheriff's business.

Disappointed, he walked to the saloon and sat back down at his table. He put the book into the backpack and sat there trying to look patient, with his hands folded in front of him. When he thought about it logically, it made sense not to go until later in the afternoon. Madison had to work until five o'clock. But his shoulders slumped, and he tried to think of other things.

Another hour crawled by. Finally, he couldn't take it anymore. It was late afternoon. Surely they would be coming for him soon. He strode out the door and walked to the livery. He brushed and saddled Jenna's horse and Josiah's horse, put their bridles on, and led them out. When Ezra walked by, Zack asked him to hold the reins while he quickly brushed Echo. It didn't take much brushing because Zack had brushed him every day since he had gotten him back. He slipped the bridle on him and led him out of his stall.

"You want me to give you a leg up, Zack?"

"I think I can do it myself, if I go on the *Indian* side." When Zack had trained Echo so many years ago, his father had insisted that he teach the horse to accept a rider mounting from the left side—the white man's way—and the right side—the Indian's way. Zack always used to mount from the right until he moved to Red Bluff and saw everyone else mount from the left. So he started mounting from the left just so he wouldn't stand out. But shortly after that, he had to give up Echo and it didn't matter anyway.

Zack grabbed Echo's mane with his right hand and swung onto the horse's back, using his left arm for balance. "I might have been able to do it before, but I didn't want to take the chance of falling and hurting myself worse!"

"Good job, Zack! Here ya go," said Ezra, handing Zack the reins of the other two horses.

As he turned the corner and trotted toward the saloon, there were Jenna and Josiah waiting out in front. "Where you been, boy? We've been waiting for you for hours!" said Josiah.

Zack started to protest when he heard Jenna laugh and saw her give Josiah a shove. "Not funny, Josiah! Not funny!"

"Thanks for bringing our horses, Zack," said Josiah.

"You knew that Madison had to work today, right, Zack? That's why we didn't hurry to get over there," said Jenna.

"I figured it out after a while," said Zack.

"Come on, now," said Josiah, after swinging up onto his horse. "Let's go get some ice cream!"

"Wait just a minute, Josiah. I need to run in and get my backpack," said Zack, as he slid off the horse and raced into the saloon. Coming back out, he slipped the backpack onto his shoulders, and then used the hitching post to climb onto Echo's back. "Let's go!"

The three rode quietly out of town and turned onto the side trail that led to the cave. When they reached the fence panel inside the cave, Josiah said, "See this, Zack? This is one of the items that helped Jenna find out who was rustlin' the cattle."

"I've seen that. Definitely doesn't belong in the nineteenth century!" said Zack. "What were the other items?"

"One was a cigarette that I found—manufactured, not

hand-rolled. And the main thing is the rustler called himself Hilary Clinton—she is a female politician in the twenty-first century." They emerged from the cave.

"Oh, yeah. That sounds familiar. I think Sarah might have mentioned that when she brought me here the first time. But I was barely conscious that day."

"Word has it, young Zack, that you could have died if Sarah hadn't brought you," said Josiah. "Are you sorry that you got a taste of the future?"

"No, I still want to live there. This GED test is my first step in making that happen. I'm hoping to start college in the fall."

"Zack, I really admire you. First the GED, then enrolling in college—in a world you never even knew existed until a couple of weeks ago. You're awesome!" said Jenna.

"Let's not make the boy conceited!" said Josiah. The three of them laughed. "Although I do think it is a wonderful, courageous thing to do, Zack. You've got grit! I'm proud of you."

"Thank you. Both of you," said Zack.

CHAPTER FORTY

MADISON WAS BESIDE herself with worry. What if Josiah and Jenna couldn't make it? What if Zack rode over on his own and they had to be alone tonight? She tried to calm herself by thinking that Jenna must have given Zack the message, because he didn't arrive Sunday. And Jenna promised that she and Josiah would be back today. Jenna understood. She wouldn't let the wrong thing happen. Jenna wouldn't have said they would definitely be here if she thought there was any doubt they would be.

After Madison was at work for an hour, Marcus came in and asked her to take a message to court again. Although she knew it was a compliment that he trusted her—because if she couldn't do it, he would get a low level attorney to do it—today, she just wanted to do something that would take her mind off her thoughts. Sitting in a courtroom waiting for a reply could be monotonous unless it was an exciting trial. She didn't know the lawyer involved, so she had no idea what to expect.

After driving to the courthouse, she walked through the security station, then into the specified courtroom and handed the message to the attorney. He was a new attorney, but he was older, and he had a good reputation. He took the message from her, nodded, and went back to his paperwork. Madison sat down at the back of the courtroom to wait.

She had walked up during a witness change. After the witness was sworn in, the man she handed the message to began his questioning. The woman was accused of being a drug runner. Madison thought that she only looked thirteen, so she would be perfect for the job. But she denied it and said she had no idea the drugs were under the passenger seat of her car. She claimed she had picked up a hitchhiker, and that he had put them there.

It was all civilized until the prosecuting attorney began hammering at the girl. Although he made her cry, the woman held her head up the entire time and answered all his questions. When Marcus's attorney asked for a redirect, he revealed that the woman had worked with a police sketch artist and had correctly identified a known drug dealer. Then the prosecutor claimed that she had seen the man's poster in the post office, and that's how she identified him.

It was dirty business. Sometimes Madison wondered if her decision to become an attorney was a good one. When she had thoughts like that, which she did occasionally have, then she told herself that she would do something benevolent like working in the public defender's office or perhaps with the local Ute or Navajo tribe.

The trial continued and didn't break for recess until almost one o'clock. The attorney brought her the message to return to Marcus.

"Wow. Great trial," said Madison. "I hope you get her

off."

"So do I," said the attorney. "You're not an attorney, are you?" he asked.

"Not yet," said Madison.

"Why don't you stay and watch the trial? You'll learn more here than you will shuffling papers back at the office."

Before Madison could protest, the man had pulled his cell phone out of his pocket and called Marcus. She heard him say, "Marcus? This is Jimmy. Yes, it's going well so far. Listen, I have," he held the phone away from his face for a second and said to Madison, "What's your name?"

"Madison."

"I have Madison here with me. I think it would be a good learning experience for her to stay. It's going to be a tough trial, but I should win. What do you say? Yes, that's what I thought, too. Okay, bye." He put the cell phone back into his pocket and said to Madison, "He agrees. You'll stay. Be back in fifty minutes. Good-bye."

And then he walked away, leaving Madison flabbergasted. Just when she had recovered her senses enough to move, the attorney turned around and walked back toward her. "I forgot to tell you. Marcus thinks you have the makings of a fine attorney and says the experience will do you good. Bye." And he turned around and walked away again.

Madison chuckled to herself. She didn't expect such a great compliment today. What a perfect week this was turning out to be! Zack was coming today, he'd pass his test tomorrow, she'd be alone with him tomorrow night, and today she got a great compliment from Marcus, who never compliments anyone! Of course, if this "Jimmy" hadn't told her what Marcus had said, she'd probably never have known. Well, thank you, Jimmy!

Since her sack lunch was back at the office and she didn't want to go back there, she decided on the healthiest fast food she could get. After finishing, she was back in the courtroom with five minutes to spare. This time, she sat down closer to the front. She noticed that Jimmy was already at his table going over his notes. He was a thorough guy and a good attorney. Madison hoped that he did win the case.

After three more hours, the trial still wasn't completed, but another recess was called until the following day. She didn't want Jimmy to call Marcus again about tomorrow, so she hurried out while he was still working at the table. If Marcus wanted her to watch the rest of the trial, he would tell her in the morning. Tonight was dinner with Josiah and Jenna *and* Zack. That is, if Jenna and Josiah rode into town with him. She felt sure they did, though. And she was glad she had been busy all day so that she hadn't had time to worry about it.

CHAPTER FORTY-ONE

MADISON PARKED HER car. When she glanced over at Jenna's two vehicles, she noticed that neither of them had moved. Without going into the barn, there was no way she could tell if Jenna, Josiah, and Zack had arrived until she stepped into the house and saw them. She closed her eyes, took a deep breath, and said to herself, "They're here. They're here. They're here." She knew that it wouldn't magically make them appear, but she felt better when she did it, and that was enough.

Confident now, she opened the front door and strolled into the house. Jenna's and Josiah's two dogs met her at the door. She smiled as she walked in. "Hello, everybody!"

Josiah sat on the couch in his usual spot, watching television and clicking through the channels. Zack sat on the other end of the couch using Madison's laptop. He looked up as she walked in. "Hi, Madison!"

"Hey, Zack, Josiah. Jenna in her room?"

"Yup," said Josiah, without looking up.

Madison walked out of the room and into Jenna's bedroom. "Thank you," she whispered to Jenna.

"It was no problem at all," said Jenna. "I told you he'd want ice cream. You ready to go? It was a busy day and neither of us had lunch."

"Sure. Just give me a few minutes to change clothes and get ready. I'll be right out." Madison hurried into her room and five minutes later hurried out again. Then she walked out to the living room where Jenna sat between Josiah and Zack.

"Oh, good. You're ready. Okay, boys, let's go," said Jenna. She put her hands on Josiah's and Zack's legs and pushed herself up.

"Oh. I don't want to go," said Zack. "I need to study for my test tomorrow."

"C'mon, Zack. You have to eat." Jenna tried to pull him up, and he wouldn't budge.

Josiah walked over and stuck out his hand toward Zack, as if to shake hands. When Zack took his hand, Josiah pulled him up and put his arm around him. "Zack, my man, you need to eat. You'll perform better on the test if you have eaten and gotten a good night's sleep. I can't help you with the sleep part, that's up to you. But I can help you with the eating part. You're coming with us. Okay?"

Madison stayed silent and watched the interaction between the two men. She wasn't sure what Zack would do.

A second later, Zack's face broke out into a smile. "You're right, Josiah. I have to eat. Let me just put the laptop away."

Josiah nodded his head. "Good enough. We'll meet you in the truck."

Jenna, Josiah, and Madison walked outside. Jenna and Madison waited while Josiah got the truck and pulled it up beside them. Zack had come out by then, and he stepped into the front seat as the two women stepped into the back.

Josiah drove a few minutes and then looked at Zack. "How about a driving lesson?"

"Yeah!" Zack, excited, leaned forward straining against the seat belt.

"Oh, come on, Josiah. I'm starved," said Jenna.

"Food can wait," said Josiah. "The man needs to learn how to drive."

Madison didn't say anything, but in her heart she could not have been happier. If Zack learned to drive—she knew he would love it—and it would be one more reason he'd want to stay in the twenty-first century. Go, Zack!

"Okay, then go to the parking lot of a big box store. That should be safe," said Jenna. "You know, Josiah. Where I taught you to drive."

"I know just the place," said Josiah.

"On second thought, wouldn't it be better to teach him in the car? It's automatic. A stick shift just makes the learning more difficult," said Jenna.

"He's a man, and he's smart, Jenna. He'll do fine. Don't worry so much," said Josiah.

Madison noticed that Zack couldn't keep still in his seat, like a kid going to a candy factory. She patted his shoulder. "You'll do great, Zack!"

A few minutes later, Josiah pulled into the large parking lot and shut off the engine. "Out, girls. This is between me and my man, Zack. Come on, Zack, switch places with me."

Madison and Jenna got out of the truck and stood to the side. Josiah and Zack got out and switched places.

Madison heard Josiah say, "Is the seat in a comfortable position for you? Can you reach the pedals without stretching? Okay, put your hand under here and you'll feel a lever. Yes! That's it. Keep moving it until you feel comfortable. Okay, let's go. First put your left foot on that left pedal down there. Yes. Keep it there. Now, turn the key. Exactly."

Madison heard the truck start. But she was disappointed when the sound from its engine kept her from hearing Josiah's instructions. She wanted to be in the truck with Zack on his first ride—to share it with him—but she also realized that it would probably make him more nervous. That's why she hadn't argued when Josiah asked her to get out.

She watched as the truck inched forward and then stalled, inched forward and then stalled, and then inched forward and kept going for several feet. "He's getting it, Jenna! He's getting it!"

Jenna laughed. "I think you're more excited than he is."

The two women watched as the truck jerked across the parking lot. After a few minutes, it started running smoothly, and Madison silently cheered him on. Too bad, though, that he couldn't get past second gear in the parking lot, she thought.

The truck headed toward them and came to a smooth stop. The engine turned off, and Madison and Jenna started clapping. Zack jumped out of the truck and dashed toward Madison. He threw his arms around Madison and hugged her. "I did it! I did it!" He swung her around. "Now, let's eat! I'm hungry!" Putting Madison back on the ground, Zack walked to the other side of the truck and climbed into the front seat.

CHAPTER FORTY-TWO

ZACK COULDN'T STOP chattering about how awesome it felt to drive the truck and how he was somehow going to find the money to buy his own. Jenna and Josiah just laughed, but Madison felt thrilled. More and more events were occurring to keep Zack here—with her. Excellent. Zack had such an excited look on his face, Madison couldn't help herself.

"Zack," she said, interrupting him. When he turned to her, she snapped his picture with her cell phone. "Thank you." Then as if nothing had interrupted him, Zack continued on about buying his own truck. He didn't stop until they received their menus at the restaurant.

Josiah and Jenna ordered Pad Thai, and Zack and Madison ordered the pineapple chicken. When the food came, Zack looked at the Pad Thai carefully. "What are you looking for, Zack?" asked Josiah.

"Matthew recommended it to me, and I just wanted to see what it looked like. I almost ordered it tonight, but the last time I had the pineapple chicken, it was so good that I had to have it again," Zack said, as he dug into the pineapple.

"Zack, did Jenna tell you that your test is Tuesday, tomorrow?" asked Madison.

"Oops, forgot to tell him that. Sorry," said Jenna.

"No, I just knew it was this week. Did you schedule just one for me?" asked Zack.

"Yes. It's the longest one. Language arts. Tomorrow at one o'clock, so you still have the morning to study," said Madison.

"Oh, language arts," said Zack.

"You're prepared, aren't you?" asked Madison.

"Yes, but I've never written anything except a few letters, and I have to write an essay for the test to demonstrate my writing skills. I'm not sure if I have any writing skills."

Jenna reached over and put her hand on Zack's arm. "You'll do fine, Zack. Don't worry."

"I know all the grammar rules really well, so the paper will be technically perfect," said Zack. "But I'm not sure if I know how to put an essay together. I'll do my best, though."

"Oh, Jenna, you'll never guess what happened today. Marcus asked me to take a message to court, and—"

Jenna interrupted Madison. "Wait. Marcus asked you to take the message? He usually gets the lower ranked attorneys to do it. Most law offices aren't like that, but Marcus is funny that way."

"I know, but he's asked me a couple of times already. Anyway, I always deliver the message and wait in the back for the attorney to bring me a reply. When the judge called a recess, the attorney told me that I'd learn a lot more watching his trial than I would shuffling papers at the office. He pulled out his cell phone, called Marcus, and asked him if I could stay!"

"What was the trial about, Madison?" asked Zack.

"A woman accused of being a drug runner."

"What's a drug runner?" asked Zack.

"That's a discussion for another time, Zack," said Jenna.

"Okay. But Madison, do you think that sometime I can watch a trial?"

"Sure, Zack. Did you want to take another test this week? I think there's another test Thursday. If you were scheduled for a test Thursday, you could go to court Wednesday to watch. It would be a good experience for you."

"Yeah, that sounds great," said Zack.

"Madison, has Marcus asked you to take his laundry since you told him no?" asked Jenna.

"Yup. And he gave me a half hour to bring it in, and a half hour to pick it up. When I told him I only needed fifteen minutes, he said to go ahead and take the half hour!"

"Great job, Madison!" said Jenna.

The easy conversation went back and forth between twenty-first-century topics and nineteenth-century topics. When they had finished dinner, Zack excused himself to go to the bathroom. Josiah said, "Zack, have you ever gone in a public place before?"

"No," said Zack.

"Be sure to use the 'Men's' room—I didn't know there was a difference, and Jenna still won't let me forget it!" said Josiah.

"Got it," said Zack.

When Zack had walked away out of sight, Josiah said, "Madison, I did you a favor. While we were alone in the truck, I mentioned how wonderful it was to take a shower, and I encouraged Zack to try it. I think I have him convinced. I also suggested that maybe he could go back to the store where he got the backpack and buy more clothes. I explained to him that people in this century have more than two sets."

"Thanks, Josiah, I appreciate that!" said Madison.

When Zack came back from the bathroom, he said, "There are some weird things in that bathroom."

"Josiah will have to explain those things to you when you're alone," said Jenna. "Right now, are you ready for dessert? Josiah can't wait to get his ice cream!"

CHAPTER FORTY-THREE

ZACK WOKE UP early feeling confident and ready to take on the world. No one else was up yet, so he decided to try the shower. He loved it—what a cool feeling having that water rush down like that. After getting dressed, he walked into the kitchen to prepare breakfast for himself and Madison. He'd been letting her cook for him, but now that he had two hands again, he thought it would be a pleasant surprise for her. Because he didn't want to serve her a cold breakfast, after the food was prepared, he waited to cook it until he heard her get up.

When he heard her door open, he started everything cooking and put bread in the toaster. Madison walked into the kitchen and saw him. "Zack! You sweetheart! You're making me breakfast! Thank you! Today is your test day. I should be making you breakfast."

"I woke up early and took a shower. It's so cool! And now that I have both my hands back, I can cook for us—unless you want to."

"Zack, I don't mind at all that you like to cook. You are welcome to do the cooking any time you want!"

Madison poured herself some coffee and sat down at

the table watching him flip the eggs. Everything smelled delicious, and when he brought everything to her, she was overwhelmed. "This is awesome! You're awesome!"

When they finished, Madison stood up. "I'll clean up today."

"You always used to clean up because I could only use one hand. My turn. You go on to work. I have plenty of time before my test."

"Yeah, but you should study some more."

"Honestly, I feel really prepared. I'll go over it one last time right before the test. But otherwise, I feel good about it."

"Okay, you've convinced me. You shouldn't have any problem walking to the test site. It's closer than the bookstore, but on a different street."

Zack smiled. "I'll find it. I'm going to walk around town first—see what other wonders are in this twenty-first century of yours."

"Okay, I'm going to work now. I know you'll pass the test, but I can hardly wait to see just how wonderfully you do! See ya soon. Bye." She leaned over and gave him a quick kiss on the mouth.

Zack smiled and watched her walk out of the room. Life just couldn't get any better than this. His upcoming test would be his first step in moving into this future of magnificent experiences and incredible possibilities.

When Zack had finished cleaning up the kitchen, Josiah and Jenna were still not awake. Although he was eager to get going and do some exploring before his test, he also wanted to say good-bye to them. Finally, he decided that he would be seeing them again soon, anyway. So after looking over his language arts study book one final time and checking the address on how to get to the test center, he left the house.

He had studied the map that he found on the internet and decided to take a different route than he had taken when he walked to the bookstore before. There were lots of new stores that he hadn't seen on the streets where he walked.

The one that caught his interest, though, was a large market. Walking in, he couldn't get over how huge it was inside. He had never been inside anything so large in his entire life. It was amazing. Starting at one end of the store, he walked up and down every aisle. The sheer number of fruits and vegetables astounded him. And so many rows upon rows of food in boxes—he had never seen food in boxes before. It didn't look real. When he reached the freezer section, the volume and variety of ice cream and frozen pies surprised him. Frozen pies? Did you eat them cold? Zack didn't think that would appeal to him. One aisle had pencils and paper and other items that you might find on a desk. He'd return to the market after the test to get some supplies.

After he finished at the market and moseyed down more streets admiring more shops, it was getting closer to test time. He found a sandwich shop and walked inside. They had so many different sandwiches that he didn't know what to choose. He finally ordered a turkey sandwich, chips, and a soft drink. Sitting in a corner booth, he enjoyed eating everything. When he finished, he asked the clerk where the nearest ice cream shop was. Luckily, it wasn't too far.

The ice cream shop, different from the one that Josiah had taken them to the previous night, had many flavors to choose from. Zack chose a double-decker with chocolate mint ice cream on the bottom and chocolate brownie on the top. Nothing was more delicious than the ice cream! Although he was tempted to get another double-decker with two new flavors, it was time to find the testing site. He was supposed to be there a half hour early.

Zack walked to the corner and studied the street signs. Then he closed his eyes and visualized the map he saw on the internet. Turning left, he walked two blocks, turned right, and walked three blocks. The building was before him. Finally. He felt confident about the test and confident that this was the start of his new life in the twenty-first century.

CHAPTER FORTY-FOUR

THE FRONT OF the building was all glass. Zack looked inside and saw computers all over the room. He smiled, took a deep breath, and stepped through the door. It was thirty-five minutes until the test, so he was a little early.

The young man at the desk smiled at Zack. "Welcome! You're the first one here! What's your name?"

"Zackary Murphy."

The man tapped the keyboard. "Oh, yes, here you are. I need a picture ID, please." He held out his hand.

Zack, confused, said, "What?"

"You know, picture ID. Identification. You have a driver's license?"

"No."

"Learner's permit? School card?"

Zack shook his head. "No, none of those."

"Sorry, man, you need picture ID before I can let you take the test. Those are the rules. You should have seen that when you registered for the test."

"I didn't—" Zack started to say and then stopped.

"Why don't you go get an ID card at the DMV?"

Zack nodded his head. He didn't know what DMV was, but knew he could look it up on the internet.

"All you need is a birth certificate. Look. I can't return your money, but when you get an ID card, you can sign up again as a retake, and it won't cost as much. Okay? Next!"

Zack stepped backwards, but someone had come up behind him. He said, "Oh, sorry," to the girl behind him and somehow made it back out the door. He leaned against the building while his head swam. There was a feeling going on in his body that he had never felt before —a heaviness that was pulling him down. His legs felt wobbly, and he was afraid that he would fall. Instinctively, he started taking deep breaths until he felt more like himself.

More people had gone through the door right in front of him. People who had ID cards—people who were allowed to take the test when he wasn't. Zack felt devastated. He wanted to walk away from the building so he didn't have to see the people going inside, but he didn't feel steady enough on his feet to move. After a few more minutes, he moved slowly away. A birth certificate. He didn't have one, and even if he did, it would be from the nineteenth century which wouldn't help him out at all here.

His life was over. If he couldn't live in the twenty-first century, he certainly could never be happy again in the nineteenth—not after what he had seen and experienced here. Not after Madison. Madison. What would he tell her? He hadn't even been able to tell her he loved her yet, and now he was leaving. Zack stumbled and put a hand on the nearest building to catch himself before falling. He had never anticipated not being allowed to take the test. What would he do now?

He continued walking down the street, breathing deeply, and as he passed the sandwich shop, an idea came to him. Backtracking a few paces, he entered the shop and ordered two more sandwiches. Then he walked back toward Madison's house until he arrived at the market that he had explored earlier. He bought some canned goods, a can opener, pens and paper, and a pint of ice cream. Walking back toward the house, he felt so empty inside that he didn't think he could ever feel whole again.

As he stepped inside, he felt relieved that the dogs didn't greet him at the door. That meant Jenna and Josiah had already left. What he had to do, he had to do alone. Retrieving his backpack from his bedroom, he put the language arts book back into it, along with what he had bought at the market and the sandwich store. Except the ice cream. Sitting in front of the television, he flipped through the channels as he savored every bite of the ice cream. The last ice cream he would ever have. Taking a deep breath that caught in his throat, he wiped away a tear that slid down his face. He couldn't believe that his life was over just that quick.

When he finished the ice cream, he put the empty carton in the garbage, washed and dried the spoon, and put it back in the drawer. Then he went back into the room he had been sleeping in, pulled the sheets off the bed, and set them on top of the machine Madison had told him washed her clothes and her sheets.

He scribbled a quick note to Madison, grabbed his backpack, walked out the door to the barn, and put the bridle on Echo. He hung his backpack on the stall door, swung up onto Echo's back, and slipped the backpack over his shoulders. Through the back of the stall and through two gates, and he was on the trail that led to the cave.

His heart felt like it would wither with disappointment. Encouraging Echo to canter, they arrived at the cave in just a few minutes. The tears flowed freely now as Zack left the twenty-first century behind him. He took one last look at what was left of the future he had planned, and he disappeared into the cave.

CHAPTER FORTY-FIVE

MADISON FELT SO good when she went to work. Zack had prepared her a fantastic breakfast and had cleaned up, too. He was the perfect man! Everything about him was exactly the way she would like it to be. And the one hang-up—him being from the nineteenth century—was about to be gone forever. She knew he would do well on the test. He was smart and well prepared. And he was awesome! She could hardly wait to get home to see how well he had done. It wouldn't surprise her if he got every question right!

Madison had barely gotten her computer powered up when Marcus came into the room. "Madison?"

"Yes?"

"Are you still planning on becoming an attorney?"

"Yes, I am."

"Jimmy is right. You can learn more from him in court. Go back to court today for as long as it takes to finish his trial. You can catch up on your work when you return. Good-bye," he said. Before she could even respond, he had walked out the door.

She gathered up her belongings and retrieved her

lunch from the refrigerator in the lunchroom. It was in an insulated container, so she hoped it would last until lunch. Then she left the office and drove over to the courthouse.

Jimmy was already in his seat with all his papers in front of him. Not wanting to disturb him, she sat down close to the front. Jimmy turned around just at that instant, saw her, smiled, and motioned her over. He patted the seat at the table next to him. "Sit here."

Madison moved, but Jimmy didn't say a word to her after that. He just kept studying his paperwork. The trial started and proceeded like the day before. After he had finished with one witness and the opposing counsel finished, Jimmy said, "Redirect, your honor," and stood up. He asked the witness one quick question and then sat back down. "I reserve the right to recall this witness, your honor." Then he leaned over to Madison and said, "See? I asked one quick question—all that I needed at this time. But I reserved the right to recall the witness later if needed. Only ask what you need to." Madison nodded her head, but she didn't think Jimmy noticed because he had already returned his attention to the trial.

Court was recessed at twelve fifteen. Jimmy said, "See you in an hour, Madison!" and walked out of the courtroom. Madison drove her car to a park and had lunch sitting under a shade tree. It felt relaxing. She realized that she had been so involved in the court case that she hadn't had a minute to think about Zack all morning. Looking at her watch, she thought that Zack was probably just arriving at the testing center. If he had a cell phone, she could text him and say, "Good luck!" But Zack didn't have one yet. After he settled into the twenty-first century, he'd have to get one. They could talk about that later.

Court resumed in exactly one hour. Jimmy nodded when Madison came in and sat down beside him. Aside from an occasional comment now and then, Jimmy focused on the trial. When the jury went out to deliberate, Jimmy turned to her and said, "And now we wait. I feel that it went well, and I don't think it will take them long to decide. I would say go get coffee and a muffin, but honestly, I think they'll be back out here in fifteen minutes." Then he went back to studying his papers.

Madison sat there absorbing every detail of the courtroom. This is where she saw her future. The judge, jury, bailiff, the courtroom itself—all players in her future reality. She liked that. She liked how being in a courtroom made her feel. And she would especially like it when she was working on her own case.

Less than fifteen minutes later, the jury stamped back into the courtroom. Jimmy turned briefly and smiled at her. He was correct. Madison hoped that someday she could read a jury like that. When the announcement came and Jimmy had won, he turned to her again, said, "Good job, Madison," and turned away to congratulate the no-longer accused.

It was four forty-five, too late to drive back to work. Madison got into her car and wished for all green lights, so she could get home sooner and find out how Zack did. The test was only an hour and a half, so he would surely be home by now. She pulled into the parking area in front of the house and rushed inside.

"Zack? Zack? How'd you do?"

No response. Maybe he was out in the barn talking to Echo and telling him how great he did on the test. That's what I would do, thought Madison. She ran out to the barn and found that Zack wasn't there. And her heart sank. Echo wasn't there, either. Maybe something had happened to Matthew or Sarah, and Zack had to return to the nineteenth century. The possibility that Zack had failed the test never crossed her mind, because she felt certain he had been fully prepared for it.

Despondent, she returned to the house to look for a note. Surely he had left a note for her. He wouldn't have just left without saying anything—no matter how much of a hurry he had been in. Zack was too responsible to do something like that. Madison searched the house. Nothing on the coffee table or by the television. The kitchen had no note. She walked into Zack's bedroom and saw that he had stripped the bed. Why would he do that? It was almost like he didn't expect to come back.

Panic set in. "Zack! Why would you leave and do this? And no note! How could you leave me hanging like this?" She felt wetness come into her eyes, but she blinked it away and walked into her room to change. There, on her desk, sat her laptop with a note on top of it. From Zack.

CHAPTER FORTY-SIX

ZACK EMERGED FROM the cave, sniffled, and wiped his tears away. This is my future, now, and I'll do the best I can with it, he thought. When he came to the end of the trail, instead of turning right toward the old Red Bluff, he turned Echo to the left. Although he didn't know exactly what he was going to do, he couldn't return to Red Bluff. At least not now. Maybe never. It wasn't like he had failed the test or anything—what had happened was out of his control. Still, he felt catawamptiously chawed up, and he didn't like that feeling at all. He needed to be alone for a while and sort everything out in his mind.

He already missed Madison and wondered if he'd ever see her again. That was what he regretted most of all. If he couldn't be a lawyer, so be it, but losing Madison hurt him in ways that he had never felt before. He'd never ask her to live with him here. As much as she loved her iPhone, laptop computer, and the rest of the miraculous things in the twenty-first century, he would never ask that of her. Shrugging his shoulders, he thought that he hated to do that to himself. Zack loved all those things, as well.

He thought they were so close to becoming a part of his life, and now they were just a sad memory. The door to his future had just slammed shut. That bothered him.

A birth certificate. Who would have thought that a simple birth certificate would ruin his chances to move to the future? Maybe he left too soon. Maybe Madison could think of a way to get one for him. No. He'd never ask her to do anything dishonest. And since he didn't have one, how else could he get one? Not to mention that even if he did have one, it would have the "wrong" dates on it. No. There was nothing he could do, and his hopes and plans were now only dreams. Bad dreams. Nightmares. And the worst part was losing Madison. He'd never get over her. She had captured his heart, and although she lived more than a hundred years in the future, he would always love her.

Miles went by. As Echo moved down the trail, Zack felt the wind blowing in his face. Against the wind. He was not only riding against the wind, but he felt like his life had come up against the wind. There was no stopping the wind, and no stopping the new direction his life had now taken: back to where he had started. Zack's tears came and went. He thought about what Josiah had said—that crying meant he had heart. A lot of good heart did him now. His heart was broken. His spirit was broken. He honestly felt like he had nothing left. "Nothing!" he screamed aloud. "Nothing!" Echo nickered in reply, which made Zack smile. "You're right, Echo. I have you, now. So I do have something."

Echo nickered again, and Zack rubbed the horse's neck. "I guess I *will* return to the twenty-first century. I can find coins to trade in that will make enough money to board you. Or maybe I can find the right coin and have enough money to buy a place and raise a few cattle. It's not like being an attorney, but at least it's something. What would you think of that, Echo? Would you like to hang around some cows?" Echo nickered, and Zack rubbed his neck again.

A few miles later, Zack found the side trace that he had been looking for and turned the horse. Not long after that, they came to the old cabin. Zack had been here not too long ago when he and the other men had come to rescue Sarah. Years ago, after his mother died, Zack and his father used to camp out here sometimes. So the memories that clung to this place were not happy ones.

He swung off the horse and dropped the reins on the ground. The hitching post had fallen down, but he knew that Echo wouldn't leave him. Opening the door of the cabin, he looked inside. The cabin was twelve feet by fifteen feet. It had two single beds in the two corners away from the door. One mattress had been taken over by mice, but the other wasn't bad. And someone—probably those outlaws that kidnapped Sarah—had left a bedroll that was in good condition. Good. At least he'd have a decent place to sleep.

In the center of the cabin was a small wood stove with burners on top and a kitchen table, which had three chairs around it. Two of them had wooden frames with rawhide strips for the seat. The rawhide on one chair had come undone and hung down to the floor. The third chair was made completely from wood. A rocking chair that looked in decent condition sat in a front corner. A ratty old broom lay on the floor under the bed, and a couple of cupboards leaned against one wall. That was it. Where was the bathroom? Zack laughed to himself.

He had gotten used to the comforts of the twenty-first century, and he would miss them.

He dropped his backpack on the good bed and went out to take care of Echo. Woods surrounded the cabin, but Zack remembered a meadow with a small stream nearby. It's why he and his father used to stay here. Back then it felt like the sad old cabin had all the comforts of home. Zack slipped the bridle off Echo and walked toward where he remembered the meadow to be. Echo followed, but when they got close, he gently pushed past Zack and ran into the meadow, kicking up his heels. Oh, that's right, thought Zack. Echo had been here with him years ago and remembered where the meadow was. It was probably the first time poor Echo had grazed in a meadow for years. At least the twenty-first century had done one incredibly good thing for him. He had his horse back.

CHAPTER FORTY-SEVEN

MADISON READ THE note through bleary eyes.

Dearest Madison,
I bet you thought I failed the test.

"No, Zack, I never thought that," she said aloud, trying to blink the tears away.

I didn't. They wouldn't let me take the test! I needed an identification card. And I need a birth certificate to get the ID card. So, it's not happening for me. I guess I can't live in the twenty-first century after all. I'm disappointed about not becoming a lawyer, but I'm more disappointed about losing you. I love you, Madison. Good-bye, Zack.

"He loves me!" Madison said aloud. "He really loves me. And I love him, too, but now he's gone. Why did this happen? What can I do?"

Madison held the note to her heart while tears flowed down her face. She let them, although she moved the note so it wouldn't get wet. She had never imagined that it would end like this—before it had even begun. And she felt bad that she had put Zack through this. Madison realized that she should have known he would need to have a picture ID to take the test. How did that get past her? She knew how it got past her. She had been so excited about Zack moving here that she had lost her sense of reason.

Now what was she going to do? How could she fix this? How could Zack possibly get a picture ID? Madison had to think about that one. There had to be a way. But being a man from the past, he might as well be an illegal immigrant. He had no identity. If you have no identity, then how do you get one? There had to be a way!

Wait! Josiah had a driver's license. How did he get that? Madison would have to ask next time Jenna and Josiah visited. But they just left. They wouldn't return for at least a week, probably two.

No, she had to find out sooner than that. She'd have to go back to the old Red Bluff to talk to Jenna or Josiah now. And she wanted to see Zack anyway. To apologize. To beg him to come back and try again.

Try again? Try what again? Until she figured out how to get him an identification card, there was no trying. How was she to get him an identification card? The key had to be Josiah, and how he got his driver's license.

She would go right away and find out. After changing her clothes, she looked outside. It would be dark soon. There was no way she could ride over there today and return while it was still light. If she spent the night, she'd be late for work tomorrow. This was the time she always got home. Madison shook her head and frowned. The soonest she could go was Friday or Saturday. That was the plan then. She hoped that Jenna or Josiah would have the answer she needed.

CHAPTER FORTY-EIGHT

WHEN ZACK RETURNED from bringing Echo to the meadow, he glanced at the old broom under the bed and thought he should sweep the cabin. The dust and dirt was so thick that he would probably stir up more than he got out, and then he couldn't sleep in here. But he had to do something. And something physical, to get out some of this anxiety that he felt right now, would be best.

Rummaging through the cupboards in the cabin, he found a hammer, an ax, and some old rusty nails. Maybe they would work, maybe not, but he intended to try. Then he walked outside and around back to where the corral was. He thought he remembered seeing a shovel there at one time; maybe it was still there. It was. Zack picked it up and took it to the front. Then he pulled the rotten upright post out of the ground. It was the reason the hitching post had fallen over. He thought he could use it for wood in the wood stove, so he leaned it up against the cabin.

Grabbing the ax, he walked over to a stand of trees, picked out a good one, and started hacking away. It was difficult work, but exactly what he needed. He wanted to get his mind off what he had lost. He wanted to chop at that tree with all his might, and when it fell, he wanted the tree to hit the ground so hard that it shook all his lost hopes and dreams out of him.

Part of him wanted the tree to fall on him. A small part, but still Zack felt the wanting of it. What was his life worth now, anyway? He couldn't have anything that he wanted. His life was shattered, and maybe his body should be, too. It was a comforting feeling, knowing he wouldn't have to feel the disappointment anymore. The idea started to appeal to him. Just then, Echo, returning from the meadow, trotted up to him and gave him a shove with his nose.

It made Zack laugh. "Hmmm, old boy. I didn't think I'd ever laugh again. You know exactly what I need and when I need it, don't you? Okay, I guess I do have something to live for. You! Now get yourself back to the meadow before this tree falls on you! Go ahead! Back to the meadow with you." Zack slapped the horse on the rump. Echo jumped, nickered, and trotted back toward the meadow.

Zack kept chopping at the tree until it was ready to fall. He had cut it so it would fall away from the cabin. One more blow, and Zack backed away. It hit the ground with a satisfying thump. He took a deep breath and sat on the downed tree. He had more work to do before it would become the new upright for the hitching post, but for now, he just needed to sit down, put his face in his hands, and have himself another good cry. So he did.

And when every last tear was cried out of him, he stood up to prepare the tree by hacking off the small branches and removing the bark. Moving toward the top of the tree, he chopped it until it was the right length.

When he had finished, it was a straight post with a **Y** at the top where he had cut off two larger branches.

He carried the post over to the front of the cabin. Using the shovel to take out dirt and rotted wood from where the old post was, he continued digging until the hole was deep enough for the new post. He placed the post inside the hole, then packed in the extra dirt that he had removed. Realizing the old rusty nails wouldn't hold the post, he searched through the cabin for some long strands of rawhide. Although he found a long strip, it needed some work before it would hold up a post.

Zack walked outside and turned toward the meadow where Echo was. Passing through the meadow to the other side, he found the small stream that he remembered. Echo followed him over and splashed in the stream, getting Zack wet.

"Echo! You could have a drink any time. Why did you have to choose right now to do it? You got me all wet!" Echo gently pushed his head against him, and Zack hugged the big horse's head. "How did I do without you for so long?" When tears came into Zack's eyes again, he pushed the horse away. "Go back to your meadow now."

The horse turned around and raced into the meadow. Then he turned around and looked at Zack. The horse raced back, turned around, and raced away again. "You want me to play with you? Okay, give me a minute here." Zack leaned down and soaked the long strand of rawhide in the water. When it had softened, Zack put it in his back pocket and looked at the horse. "Okay, Echo. You ready?"

The horse nickered and ran farther into the meadow with Zack chasing behind him. When the horse had slowed, and Zack had caught up to him, Zack turned around and raced back toward the stream. Echo followed at a polite distance. The two of them ran up and back several times before Zack said, “Okay, Echo, enough playing. I have to go back to work.” He stroked the horse’s neck and walked back toward the cabin.

CHAPTER FORTY-NINE

BACK AT THE cabin, Zack picked up the horizontal log that had fallen down and propped it up on the **Y** part of the new post. Then he wrapped the wet rawhide around the two sections of wood several times until it held the horizontal log firmly in place. When the rawhide dried, it would hold the bar—for at least as long as Zack would be here.

How long would he be here? Zack couldn't answer that question. Zack didn't even know why he had come to the old cabin, except that he felt he couldn't face the old Red Bluff again. It wasn't like he had failed—he knew he hadn't. It was more like the world had failed him, and that bothered him. He didn't want to talk to his friends about how his dreams had been shattered. He didn't even want to think about that right now. Perhaps that was why he had come here. So he didn't have to think about it.

After chopping the tree down, running through the meadow with Echo, and repairing the hitching post, Zack felt hungry. Taking one sandwich out of his backpack, he unwrapped it and ate it. Then, from his backpack, he took out the other sandwich and the other food that he had bought at the market and set everything on the dusty table. He'd deal with the dust tomorrow. If he wanted this food to last, he needed to conserve it for as long as possible.

He knew that he shouldn't have eaten the second sandwich today. But after going through what he considered hell, he deserved the extra sandwich and the ice cream. How would he go on without ice cream? It was so delicious! No wonder Josiah insisted on going to the future every couple of weeks. Zack couldn't blame him for that. But there were more important things than ice cream for Zack to think about right now.

Reaching into his backpack, he pulled out the language arts book to go over it again. Opening the book, he began flipping through it and reading random parts. He knew it thoroughly and could practically recite it chapter by chapter and even word for word. Why was he even wasting time going over this material? Any possibility of life in the twenty-first century had evaporated along with the ID card that he didn't have and couldn't get. Angry with himself and his situation, he threw the book across the room, and tears came into his eyes.

"No!" he shouted as he rubbed the tears away. "No! I won't cry anymore over what I can't change!" Zack knew that if he was ever to find happiness he would either have to figure out how to change the outcome of what had happened or learn to accept it. Changing it didn't seem like an option. If it *was* an option, it was out of his realm of possibility. He didn't know enough about the future to understand all its subtleties and possibilities yet.

Maybe Madison could figure out a way to get him an ID card. Maybe Zack should have talked to Madison before he left. But he couldn't bear that. Exhaling slowly, he thought he still had a few days to give it all some thought. Seeing the food spread out across the table, he realized that it wouldn't last long—certainly not long enough to get him through the weekend, unless he was really, really careful. He nodded his head. Careful and hungry, that is. Careful and hungry.

After gathering the food and putting it into a cupboard so he didn't have to see it, he picked up the language arts book and brought it back to the kitchen table. He had had enough of that. Opening the backpack, he pulled out the rest of the books that were inside. Science, math, and social studies. What was this? The John Grisham novel! Zack hadn't had a chance to read much of it because he had been so busy studying for the GED test. Now, he had time to sit down, relax, and read a good novel. It was getting later in the day, and the sun was starting to go down. He had never thought to get candles while he was at that market. Did they even still use candles in the future?

If he was back in the twenty-first century, he could just flick on the light switch. He missed the conveniences there. More than that. He missed Madison. A lot. He missed her so much that his heart hurt. It was a longing deep inside him like a piece of himself was missing.

CHAPTER FIFTY

OUTSIDE, LEANING AGAINST a tall tree, Zack read the Grisham novel until it was too dark to see. Then he walked into the old cabin and fell asleep. In the dark—with no candles—what else could he do? Next morning, he lay in bed thinking about life in the cabin. No conveniences at all. Even the old Red Bluff had more conveniences than the cabin. The composting toilet in his room above the saloon wasn't as good as a regular bathroom in the twenty-first century, but it was better than going in the woods. Could he be happy living in the nineteenth century after experiencing the twenty-first? Granny, Jenna, Sarah, and Ryan had all moved from there and were perfectly happy. And they had grown up with all the conveniences.

So why did he feel so deprived when he thought about staying in the past? Because in a strange way, he didn't feel like he belonged here anymore. Truth of it was, he hadn't felt like he belonged here in a long time. He was the only Indian in town. Although his friends completely accepted him as just another man, it wasn't only the range cowboys who gave him a hard time. He had overheard some of the town's people referring to him as "chief" behind his back. Zack had always been an outsider and had always felt different.

The twenty-first century was different. When he was there, he felt accepted, comfortable, and free from the prejudice of the nineteenth century. While he was sure that some of that still existed in the twenty-first century, it wasn't as "acceptable" as it was in the nineteenth. That's where he wanted to make his life. That's where he wanted to get married and raise a family—in a place where his children could grow up proud of what they were and not ashamed of it.

Zack needed to go back and find a way to stay there. He wasn't ready to hang up his fiddle just yet. If it was not possible to stay there, he could still search for the valuable coins, trade them in, and somehow get enough money to go to college here in the nineteenth century. No, it would not be as satisfying and he would not be as happy. And most important, he would not have Madison, but at least he wouldn't be sitting around in a saloon, reading books, and dreaming of the good life. No, Zack was the kind of man who needed to do something about it. He had sat in that saloon for far too long already. Now—nineteenth century or twenty-first century—he would make something of himself.

He stretched, got out of bed, and regretted that he hadn't thought to buy some eggs so he could have a decent breakfast—not that they would have survived the long horseback trip over here—but they still would have made a good breakfast. Zack decided that although he had made his decision, he needed to "get back to the earth" and stay in the rustic cabin until his food ran out so he could overcome the bad feelings that had overcome him. Looking over his food supplies, he thought that if he really stretched and was really careful, he could make it last until Saturday. He'd be starving by then, but he'd have a little to eat every day.

So the decision was made. He would head back to the old Red Bluff Saturday. He imagined that Madison would be there. If she felt the same way about him as he felt about her, she would be there. And he didn't want her—or anyone—to worry about him. Because she had to work through Friday, she probably wouldn't arrive until Saturday. So he would ride in Saturday and see if she had come up with a way to get him a picture identification. Until then, he'd spend his days reading, studying, and contemplating life.

CHAPTER FIFTY-ONE

FRIDAY COULDN'T COME soon enough for Madison. After spending Monday and Tuesday in court all day with Jimmy, the rest of the week was busywork—typing, filing, and answering phones. It kept her mind occupied, though, so thoughts of Zack were minimal. Although every night when she arrived home and walked into the barn and saw where he had kept Echo, the pain of his absence all came rushing back to her.

Everything hinged on how Josiah got his driver's license. Her whole world depended on that information.

Madison rushed home from work, changed clothes, grabbed her already packed backpack, ran out to the barn, brushed Chaco, and was on his back and through the gates in record time. She had decided to go Friday night instead of waiting until Saturday morning for one reason: she couldn't wait to get there and make sure Zack was okay. So, now she was on her way, trotting down the trail toward the cave—and toward Zack.

Seeing the Red Bluff sign made her feel a little better. She was closer to seeing Zack and getting the information from Josiah. Everything would be fine. Although she knew that, she didn't feel very calm or very convinced. What if Zack couldn't do what Josiah did? What if whatever it was wouldn't work for Zack? What if what if what if? And all bad things. She thought maybe she should try what if happy statements. What if Zack could get a driver's license just like Josiah? What if Zack came to live with her? What if Zack attended the same college she did and they could talk about lawyerly stuff together? Yes, that was better. Madison took a deep breath and decided to take Chaco straight to the livery before checking in at the hotel.

After dropping off Chaco with Ezra, instead of going to the hotel, she walked directly to the saloon. She had to see Zack, and she couldn't wait. Madison pushed through the swinging doors with wide-eyed anticipation of seeing Zack. It was late enough that Sarah was already at the piano, but she had just finished a song and motioned Madison over to her.

"So how did our boy wonder do? Did he ace the test?"

Madison's smile drooped, and she felt all the blood rush out of her head. Grabbing the piano for support, she managed to wheeze out, "You mean he's not here?"

"What do you mean, 'here'? We thought he was with you!" Sarah stood up concerned and left Madison grasping the piano. Madison watched as she strode quickly across the saloon and behind the bar to talk to Matthew. He looked up at Madison and rushed over to her.

"Where's Zack?" he asked.

"I thought he was here," said Madison, feeling more stable on her feet now. "I came here to see him."

"What happened?" asked Sarah, who stood right behind Matthew. "We know Zack. There's no way he didn't pass the test."

"He never took the test," said Madison. "He needed a picture ID and didn't have any. That was my fault. I should have known that."

Sarah stepped forward. "Don't blame yourself, Madison. Coming from the future to the past is not a problem. But Zack's the first one who came from the past into the future. There's bound to be problems. You'll solve it. Don't worry." She patted Madison's hand.

"I hope so, Sarah. I hope so," said Madison.

"We need to go look for him," said Matthew. "Make sure he's all right."

Sarah turned Matthew around to face her. "Matthew, Zack is a man. He probably just needs some space. I know how much he wanted to move to the future, and this must have been terribly disappointing to him. I don't blame him for wanting to get away for a while. You need to leave him be, Matthew."

Matthew grunted, turned, and walked back behind the bar, sullen. Sarah and Madison watched him go. Then Sarah turned back to Madison. "Stay here tonight. You don't need to go to the hotel. You can stay in a room upstairs. It might make you feel better."

"I need to go see Josiah. Find out how he got his driver's license. If Zack could get a driver's license, everything would be fine."

"I don't know if he'd be there this late," said Sarah. "Now that Rawlins is always sober, Josiah has been leaving early to go home to Jenna. But you can try. You never know. Sometimes he stays late if something is going on."

"I have to try," said Madison.

"Here," said Sarah. "I'll take your backpack up to your room. You go ahead and check on Josiah." Sarah took the backpack, and Madison watched as she disappeared up the back stairs.

Madison walked slowly out of the saloon. She felt as if her whole life depended on Josiah's answer. As she glanced down the street, she saw Jenna heading into the sheriff's office. Oh, good, thought Madison. They're still here. I'll know in a minute.

Gathering speed and taking a deep breath to give her courage, she walked into the sheriff's office. Josiah was at his desk talking to a rancher, and Jenna was standing on the opposite side of the room looking at wanted posters. Jenna turned as Madison walked in.

"Hey, Madison," she said warmly. "How'd Zack do on the test? Knowing Zack, he probably got every question right!"

"Hi, Jenna, no. He never took the test. That's why I came here to talk to you. Zack couldn't take the test because he didn't have a picture ID."

Before Madison had a chance to say anything more, the rancher left the office, and Josiah walked over. "Hi, Madison! How'd Zack do?"

"He couldn't take the test, Josiah, because he didn't have a picture identification. How'd you get your driver's license? That's Zack's only chance," said Madison.

"Oops," said Jenna.

"I, uh, well, your auntie here convinced me, a man of the law, that I didn't need a driver's license as long as I didn't get caught. So I never got one. What would they do to me if they caught me? Not let me drive anymore? Fine, I'll go back to my horse. Or, let Jenna drive, of course."

"Oh," said Madison, disappointed. "That was my only hope—that if you had a driver's license, then Zack could get one, too. Then he could take the test."

"I never thought of that, Madison," said Jenna. "No, with all the new rules and regulations, I don't know how anyone from the past could get any kind of ID card. I'm sorry, honey." Jenna put her hand on Madison's face. "You'll figure something out. I know you will."

Madison turned to leave. "I don't have any idea what it would be, Jenna. This was my only hope."

CHAPTER FIFTY-TWO

MADISON HAD A horrible night's sleep. She was in the room next to Zack's room, and every time she heard the slightest noise, she woke up thinking it was him. But it was just old building noises, and then she had to struggle to get back to sleep. And sleeping came after spending hours in the saloon, jumping every time someone came through the door. But none of them had been Zack.

She had no idea where he could be and wondered why he had disappeared. There was no way he could feel ashamed at what had happened. It was beyond his control. More than likely, he was extremely disappointed and needed to be alone for a while. Madison understood that. She was disappointed, also. Now she also felt sick to her stomach, but she knew she wasn't sick. It was just that she felt hopeless—it didn't seem there was any way at all to get Zack a picture ID. And if he couldn't get an ID, then he couldn't take the test and couldn't get into college—which meant he wouldn't move to the twenty-first century and they couldn't be together.

She dragged herself out of bed and somehow managed to get dressed without weeping. When she heard

Sarah and Matthew walk by and head downstairs, she thought that eating something might settle her stomach and make her feel better. So she slowly walked downstairs, exhaling deeply, and feeling sorry for herself. And she knew she shouldn't. Zack had a lot more to feel sorry for himself about. He had just lost the future that he had planned. Still, that didn't make her feel any better, so she sighed, plastered a smile on her face, and walked into the back room where Matthew was cooking breakfast.

"Hi, Sarah. Hi, Matthew."

"Hi, Madison! Sleep well?" asked Sarah.

"I woke up every time I heard a noise that I thought might be Zack."

"He'll be back, don't worry," said Sarah.

"I hope you're right," said Matthew. "He's never disappeared like this before."

Madison sighed and looked down. "He's never lost a future that he had hoped for, before. But Zack is resilient. He'll come out of this okay. I know he will." She didn't know that, but she hoped he would.

The three of them heard the front doors open. It was too early for customers. Before anyone could stand up and investigate, Zack came bursting into the room. "Good morning, everybody! I'm starved!" He put his arm around Madison, kissed her on the mouth, and pulled up a chair beside her.

"Where have you been, young man?" asked Sarah sternly, making everyone laugh and breaking the tension.

"I rode out to the old cabin. You know the one," said Zack.

"You mean, *that* cabin?" asked Sarah.

"That's the one," said Zack.

"What'd you go out there for?" asked Matthew.

"I needed to get away, be by myself, think about my life. Madison told you what happened?"

"Yes, but none of us could figure out why you ran away. You had nothing to be ashamed of." Sarah put a plate of eggs in front of him and squeezed his shoulder.

Zack shook his head slowly from side to side. "No, it wasn't ashamed. I felt frustrated about what happened. It was a barrier to what I wanted: moving to the twenty-first century." He turned to Madison. "Is there a way I *can* get a picture identification?"

"Oh, I came here to talk to Josiah to find out how he got his driver's license. I thought that was the key," said Madison.

"He doesn't have a driver's license," said Zack. "He told me that when we were driving in the parking lot."

"Yeah, now I know that." She looked at Zack and frowned. "I'm all out of ideas, Zack. I'm sorry. I should have anticipated that you would need ID to take the tests and get into school. I just didn't think about it—I didn't want to think about it. I'm sorry."

Zack patted her hand. "It's okay, Madison. I'm not blaming you. What does a picture ID look like, anyway?"

Madison reached into her pocket and pulled out a bunch of cards. As she went through her school ID, library card, and credit cards, looking for her license, one card dropped out on the floor. Finding her license, she handed it to Zack and then stooped over to pick up the fallen card. As she was about to shove it into the pile with the rest, she held it out in front of her. "Zack! This is it! This is how you'll get an ID!"

Zack handed her back her license and took the card in her hand. He read the front of the card, "Madison Two Feathers is an official member of the Oglala Sioux Tribe.

Nice picture, Madison. But how will this ID do me any good. I don't look like you! And I'm Navajo."

"No, not *my* card! We'll get *you* a Navajo Nation ID card!"

"How are we going to do that?" asked Zack.

"There's an office not too far from Red Bluff," said Madison.

"How will they know that I'm really Navajo and not just saying that?" asked Zack.

"He's right, Madison. It will be the same problem there. No birth certificate," said Sarah.

"No! It's the twenty-first century! I bet they'll accept DNA testing!" said Madison.

"What's DNA? And how can I even take the test without ID?" asked Zack.

"Your DNA is part of you, Zack. Everyone has different DNA. They can test you with blood or saliva and I think hair, too. I know they can test dogs to find out their heritage, and this is the same thing. It has to work! It just has to!" said Madison. "Will you at least try it, Zack? Will you try?"

Zack smiled at Madison. "Sure, Madison. I'll try it. I have nothing to lose, right?"

"Great! You can come back with me tonight, and we'll go Tuesday afternoon. When I go to work Monday, I'll ask for Tuesday afternoon off. It won't be a problem. Then we'll go and take care of it! Get you an ID card!"

Zack took Madison's hand and looked into her eyes. "I'm not coming back with you, Madison. This is where I belong for now. Echo and I will ride over Tuesday and meet you at the house in the afternoon. Okay?"

Madison looked at Zack. She thought how this experience had changed him. He was more assertive now—

more sure of himself. The change bothered her in a way, but she thought she liked it. She nodded her head. "Okay, Zack, Tuesday afternoon then."

CHAPTER FIFTY-THREE

TUESDAY MORNING ARRIVED, and Zack felt relieved. He honestly didn't think anything would come of Madison's attempt to get him a tribal ID. DNA. He didn't know what kind of newfangled thing it was, but surely his traditional tribe would not accept it. But to please Madison, and to assure himself that it would not work, he said he'd try. Although to be honest, he had his own reasons for returning to the twenty-first century.

As he and Echo rode through the cave to the future, Zack wondered how many more times he'd come through that cave. At least once. He knew that. No matter what happened today at the tribal office, he needed to return at least one more time. Although Zack had planned to study his coin book Sunday and go to the bank Monday, Matthew had needed him both days. It made Zack feel good helping again. But he had thought that if he went through a bunch of coins at the bank, surely he would find some that were worth something. Maybe he'd even find the one that Stan, the coin guy, had requested. A 1795 silver dollar. It would mean a lot of money. And he needed a lot of money regardless of which direction his future lay.

He arrived at Madison's barn at midmorning. After removing Echo's bridle and making sure he had food and water, Zack walked into the house, which wasn't locked. Madison had said that most people always locked their houses, but she lived far enough out that she never locked the doors. Zack picked up Madison's laptop from her bedroom and carried it into the living room.

Opening a Google search screen, he googled "law schools in the 1800s." He didn't have much time for research, so it might not be complete, but he found four law colleges, all of them on the east coast. That disappointed him, but he'd do what he had to do. Zack wasn't sure he could count on the accuracy of something so long ago, but it said the first year tuition was eighty dollars! With the right coins, he could easily come up with that much. After scribbling down the addresses—he felt certain that even if they weren't exact, his letters would get there—he closed the laptop and returned it to Madison's room.

Then he grabbed the nearly empty backpack he had brought, slipped it over his shoulders, and walked into town. Madison shouldn't be home for more than an hour. If he hurried, he had plenty of time for the bookstore, the coin shop, and the thrift store. Fifteen minutes later, he arrived at his first stop, the bookstore. Although he didn't have much confidence in getting a tribal membership card—just in case—he wanted to be prepared for living in the twenty-first century. So he bought himself several vocabulary books. His nineteenth-century vocabulary was sorely lacking for a twenty-first-century education. And even if he ended up back in the nineteenth century, it didn't hurt to be more learned. He also bought a few more John Grisham novels.

Next stop was the thrift store, and they were having a sale. You could buy everything you could fit in a paper bag for only five dollars. Zack managed to stuff in five pairs of jeans and seven shirts, a belt, and a small backpack. All of that was put into his old backpack along with his new books.

Then he walked to the coin store and stepped in. "Hello, Stan," he said when he saw the man behind the counter.

"Hi, Zack. Are you buying or selling today? Or both? Did you find me that 1795 'Silver Plug' that I'm still looking for?"

"No, not yet. I haven't had a chance to do much research since the last time I saw you," said Zack. "Can you tell me if any of these are worth anything?" That morning, before leaving, he had gathered up all the coins in his room. He didn't recognize the dates on them, and he trusted Stan.

Stan took the coins and turned them over in his hands. "Most of them aren't worth much—especially if you're going to trade them back for quarters and half dollars. I'll give you five hundred for this one. And I ordered some more quarters and half dollars if you want more of those."

Zack picked out thirty-seven half dollars and nineteen quarters. "How much for these?"

"Well, with the five hundred for this one," he held up the coin that Zack had given him, "how about a thousand dollars?"

"That sounds good." Zack reached into his pocket and counted out the money for Stan.

"Do you always carry that much cash on you?" asked

Stan. "Red Bluff is usually a safe place, but there are people out there—"

"Not usually, but I knew I was coming here today," said Zack. "Stan, besides the 1795 silver dollar that you're looking for, are there any other coins that are worth a lot of money?"

"Most overdate coins are worth something."

"What's 'overdate'?" asked Zack.

"You're not really a coin collector, are you, son?"

"No, it was my grandfather," said Zack easily.

"You need to get yourself a good book on coins and look up overdate. That's when a coin was stamped with one date and then stamped with another date on top of it. Most coins like that are pretty valuable. Any time there is something 'different' about a coin—it's worth more."

"Thanks, Stan," said Zack. "I appreciate the help and the information. I'll come see you again—I hope with at least one of those special coins."

CHAPTER FIFTY-FOUR

ZACK STARTED WALKING back to Madison's house. As he walked through a residential neighborhood close to the house, a car pulled up beside him.

"Hey, handsome. Want a ride?"

"You bet, pretty lady!" said Zack, as he opened the door and sat beside Madison.

"Your backpack looks heavy! What's in it?" asked Madison.

"Some books and a bunch of new clothes."

"You can drop them at the house. I need to change before we go. Are you looking forward to this?"

"Sure! Let's find out if it's the answer."

"I hope it is," said Madison quietly. "I really hope it is."

After Zack dropped off his heavy backpack and Madison changed her clothes, they returned to the car. "It will take almost an hour to get there. You ready for a road trip?"

"Whatever it takes, Madison. It doesn't matter, though. I'm always happy when I'm with you." Zack looked at her lovingly, aware that this might be their last time together. But he didn't allow himself to think like that. He couldn't.

After a lively hour of listening to the radio and talking about the law, school, GED and SAT tests, picture identification, and the limitations of the nineteenth century, they were almost there. They had passed a sign that said, "Welcome to the Navajo Nation!" Just after that, Zack pointed out another sign that said "Diné Bikayah." Navajo Lands. He knew that Diné didn't mean Navajo. It meant "the people."

Madison pulled onto a narrow, paved road. Then Zack saw an incredible building with a sign in front that said "Diné Tribal Office." The building was made of red clay brick like he had seen when he was a kid traveling with his father. And it had wooden posts going through the top of the pillars in front to the main building. Although it was magnificent, Zack wondered why it wasn't in the shape of the traditional hogan, which he had lived in when he was very young.

When they stepped out of the car, Zack could tell that Madison felt nervous, but he didn't. Either it would work or it wouldn't. Although he wanted to stay in the twenty-first century with Madison and go to college here, he had come to the place where he could accept it either way. He thought that was a good place to be. So he smiled at Madison, grabbed her hand, and opened the big red door for her.

Following Madison in and looking around, Zack walked briskly up to the office window. A young woman with long, black braids and a shy smile was on the other side. She was Diné. He recognized the features. His people. Madison was Indian, but she was Sioux and looked different. He introduced himself to the woman in

Diné and explained what he needed.

"I'm sorry," she said. "I don't speak Navajo. My grandmother tried to teach me, but it didn't take." She shrugged her shoulders. "Speak English, please."

That confused Zack. She didn't speak Diné? More had changed than he had realized. "My name is Zack Murphy, born out of the Bitter Water Clan. My father, Isaac Murphy, is white. I'd like to get a Tribal Membership Card."

The young woman turned to her computer. "What's your mother's name?"

"Johona Benali."

The woman clicked away at her keyboard. "I'm not finding her, Zack. Was she a member of the tribe?"

"Yes," said Zack.

"Do you know if she was officially registered?"

"That I don't know," said Zack.

Madison stepped forward. "When did the official register begin?" she asked.

"1940," said the young woman.

"Oh, okay," said Zack, as he turned away from the window, disappointed.

"Wait," said Madison, stepping up to the window. "Do you do DNA testing?"

"DNA testing? Oh, no. Your mother or father has to be an enrolled member of the tribe before you can enroll. Sorry," she said, as she turned away from the keyboard and picked up the cell phone that was beside her.

Zack was out the door before Madison, taking big strides back to the car. Madison had to run to catch up to him. "I'm sorry, Zack. I'm so sorry. I was sure they would accept DNA testing. It's the newest thing."

"My people are traditional people, Madison. I didn't know what DNA testing was, but I didn't think it was something they would adopt so casually."

When Madison unlocked the car, he climbed into it. He looked out the side window, because he didn't want her to see the tears in his eyes. He thought he could handle it no matter what happened. But he couldn't. Again, he felt as if he had lost everything that was important to him—law school in the twenty-first century and Madison.

CHAPTER FIFTY-FIVE

ZACK WAS SO quiet on the way home that Madison had plenty of time to think. At first, she tried talking to him, but when he continued to stare out the side window and give her one or two word answers, she realized that he needed some time alone. So she didn't say anything more —just hoped that he wouldn't turn her way and see the tears falling silently down her face.

They stopped at a fast food place on the way home, and although he ate a lot, he was still reluctant to talk. A few more minutes down the road, however, he said, "I still can't believe that woman didn't know how to speak Diné. Is that what it's come to in the twenty-first century? Native people not knowing their own language, their own customs? That's horrible."

"A lot has happened in the last century, Zack. Many native people are ashamed of who they are. My own mother—she's not native, but her husband was—anyway, she won't use his last name. She says she's not ashamed, but it still bothers me."

Zack shook his head and then continued looking out the window. Madison didn't want to push him, but she was afraid of losing him, and she didn't want that to happen. And although something inside her gut was telling her to be silent and let it go, she couldn't help herself and had to speak. "Zack, I know this didn't work out, but there are other ways we can do this."

"You mean there's another way to get an ID card?" he asked, suddenly animated again.

"Well, no. But you know there are thousands of illegal aliens who have sneaked into this country, and they live perfectly normal lives here."

"Normal except they have to stay away from the law? Didn't we watch a movie where someone was deported when they caught him? Madison, I want to be a lawyer, not someone who runs from the law. If there's no way I can get an ID, then that's it. It's finished. I have to accept that, and you do, too."

Madison wanted him to ask her to move back to the nineteenth century with him. She wouldn't do that—couldn't do that. There was no possibility of her ever moving back there—even for Zack. But she really wanted him to ask—so she knew that he cared for her as much as she cared for him.

When they arrived home, it was almost dark. Madison followed when Zack walked into the house. She watched as he picked up his backpack and slid it on over his shoulders. Before he had a chance to turn around and head toward the door, Madison said, "Zack, it's getting dark. Just stay here tonight."

He turned toward her and looked into her eyes. "Madison, it's no use. I can't move here. As much as I want to be here with you and become a lawyer in the twenty-first century, it's not possible. Let's just let it go."

Zack took a step toward the door, and she put her

hand on his arm and turned him back toward her. "I don't want to let it go, Zack."

"We have no choice, Madison. We have no choice."

"Stay here tonight, Zack."

"No. I can still make it through the cave before dark."

"Spend the night with me, Zack."

Zack took a step backward and looked at her. "No. No, Madison, I can't do that."

She held onto his arm. "Stay with me tonight, Zack. I want you to."

Madison noticed that although he shook his head, no, his demeanor had softened—his body turned toward her instead of toward the door. "No, I shouldn't."

"Zack, please. For me."

Zack looked down. "Are you sure that's what you want? Are you sure, Madison?"

"Yes, I'm sure." She put more pressure on his arm and pulled him toward her. After they kissed, a long, satisfying kiss—their first—Zack followed her into the bedroom and closed the door.

CHAPTER FIFTY-SIX

MADISON LAY ON the bed crying hysterically—the kind of crying where you can barely catch your breath between sobs. It scared her, but she felt that she needed to cry it out, and that she would ultimately be okay.

After Zack left early in the morning, she had somehow managed to hold herself together long enough to call the office and say that she was sick. Never in her life had she called in sick before when she wasn't sick. Now wasn't any different. She was sick—at heart. It felt like she would never recover from the emptiness she now felt. She'd survive the violence of the sobbing, but she wasn't sure at all that she would survive the heartache.

Zack had been a gentleman, although he had insisted on leaving before breakfast. He said he couldn't handle the loss—that he almost had it all and now everything was lost to him. He had told her that he loved her, several times. And before he walked out the door and kissed her good-bye, he had put his hands on her shoulders, looked into her eyes, and said ardently, "I will love you, forever. *Forever*."

And now he was gone from her *forever*. There was

nothing she could do about it. No amount of wishing or hoping could get him a birth certificate or an ID card. A fake one? She had considered that. It would probably work to get him the GED test, but when it came around to show the ID for college, she didn't think it would work. If he could successfully take the GED test, then he would be even more frustrated that he couldn't get into college.

Zack, coming from the past with no traceable paperwork, was a nonentity. Although she loved him dearly, she felt she was too young to get married. Still, before she broke down completely that morning, she had done an internet search to see if he could become a citizen if she married him. The website she found, full of legal jargon, said that at some point in the process, he had to return to his "home country." Yeah, right. This *was* his home country! Just not his home time. No. She had gone over it and over it in her head. There was no feasible way to get him a legal birth certificate or an identification card. Which meant—there was no way for them to be together.

The thought of that sent her back into racking sobs. As much as she hated the thought, there was only one obvious solution to the problem. She had to go back to the nineteenth century to be with Zack. Losing her cell phone, her iPad, her laptop computer—as much as she loved her modern technological devices—they meant nothing to her without Zack in her life. It seemed the most logical solution; and yet, her electronics would not be all that she would lose. She wasn't positive, but she didn't think that law schools in the nineteenth century would even admit women for several more years. So what would she do in the nineteenth century? Zack could go to law school, and she would—what? Do the laundry and the cooking? It didn't matter. All that she was and all that she wanted meant nothing if she couldn't have him.

It was decided then. She would quit her job, give up everything she had been, everything she had known, to return to the nineteenth century to be with Zack. The thought was somewhere between comforting and disturbing. It made the sobs start all over again.

CHAPTER FIFTY-SEVEN

ZACK COULDN'T REMEMBER exactly when he made the decision. Was it before he reached the cave or on the old Red Bluff side of the cave? It didn't matter. The decision was made, and that was that. He couldn't let Madison move to the nineteenth century. And he knew that she would. He could see it in her eyes when he said good-bye to her. His desire to become a lawyer was always just a pipe dream anyway. Until he had found out about the cave and the twenty-first century, he never thought it would really happen. Yes, he had read and reread that silly Pennsylvania law book, but he didn't really believe he could become a lawyer.

The whole GED test and going to college in the future, it was something nice to hold onto, but it wasn't realistic. He was a nineteenth-century man and couldn't expect to go into the future, go to college, and become a lawyer.

But he could go to the future and *not* become a lawyer. If he didn't need the GED test, then maybe he could get away with not having a birth certificate and picture ID. He had to try. Zack laughed to himself. He wouldn't know where they'd deport him to if they caught him anyway! Regardless, he had made up his mind. He'd return to the twenty-first century to be with Madison. Half his dream would come true. He'd have Madison. That was more important than becoming a lawyer anyway. And he would immediately start putting his plan into motion.

Since he had left without breakfast, Zack was hungry when he walked into the saloon. He felt grateful that Sarah and Matthew had already finished—he didn't want to talk to either of them right now. After fixing himself some breakfast and eating it as fast as he could, he took two stairs at a time up to his room.

He unpacked his backpack and left the clothes that he had bought on the bed. There wasn't enough room in the chest of drawers for everything. No matter. He wouldn't be here that much longer. Taking out his pen and paper and picking up the coin book from the top of the chest of drawers, he sat down on the bed to work.

Two hours later, he had a long list of coins that were worth a lot of money—several thousand dollars up to fifty thousand dollars. One was worth more than eighty thousand. Another was worth a million—the one Stan had mentioned to him—but he didn't count on finding that one. Although maybe he'd get lucky and find one of those worth thousands. He stuck the paperwork in his pocket, gathered all the old coins that he had, and counted them. Only fifty dollars, but it should be enough to do what he needed.

He ran downstairs, eager to complete his "job." It may not be as satisfying as becoming a lawyer, but if he was successful at it, he and Madison could live like kings. And there were several coins coming out in the early 1870s that were worth a lot of money. If he could find those before they had too much wear on them, it would be a good profit for him and Madison.

Zack walked into the bank and up to the teller. After plunking twenty dollars on the counter, he said, "I'd like to have twenty dollars worth of pennies, please. And could I sit in a back room to look at them?"

The man behind the counter put the coins in a tray and handed it to Zack. "Look at them? What for?"

"Oh, sorry. I just need a table. Do you have one I could use?"

The man led Zack and his tray full of pennies to a room with a large table and several chairs set around it. "This is perfect," said Zack. "Thank you."

Zack sat down, hauled out his notes, and began going through the pennies. Most of them, he could look at the date on the front. But he needed to turn some coins over so he could examine them carefully. When he had finished, forty-five minutes later, he had one penny picked out that might be worth two thousand dollars. It wasn't exactly what he had hoped for. He replaced it with one of his own.

Carrying the tray back to the teller, he asked if he could have another twenty dollars of pennies. When the man looked at him as if he was nuts, Zack added, "Different pennies, please."

The man took the tray from him, shook his head, and started walking away. Then he turned back to Zack and said, "I'll bring them to you."

Zack walked back to the room and stuffed his paperwork in his pockets. While he waited, he mused on what he was doing: using a twenty-first-century coin book in a nineteenth-century bank to find coins that were valuable enough so he could live comfortably in the twenty-first century. It was crazy.

The world of coin collecting was a world unto itself. Coins were classified as to how sharp and unblemished the image on them was. If the rim of the coin was well defined and the image visible, it could be classified as very good. If the image was still shiny with no major flaws, then it could be classified as choice proof. Those were worth the most.

For a modern collector, choice proof would be almost impossible to find. But being in the nineteenth century had its advantages. He still might find some choice proof coins. At least ones from the last couple of years. Despite that he had only found one coin worth saving in the twenty dollars of pennies, Zack thought this method of looking for valuable coins could work.

The man brought Zack another tray of pennies and dropped it on the table in front of him. Some coins jumped but did not escape the tray. Zack looked at him and said, "Thank you." The man didn't reply and exited the room. Ignoring him, Zack began the long process of going through each coin.

CHAPTER FIFTY-EIGHT

MADISON DIDN'T KNOW how long she had lain there, sobbing, when her mother stepped into the room. Kat walked over, sat on the edge of the bed, and put her hand on Madison's forehead before saying anything. "Are you okay? Your temperature feels normal."

Madison pushed her hand away. "I don't have a fever."

"Then what's wrong? Why did you call in sick? Why are you in bed?"

"How did you know I called in sick?"

"I called you at work, and they told me. Now tell me, what's wrong?"

"It's Zack," said Madison.

Madison's mother, Kat, wasn't the most doting of parents, but she could act like a mother bear if provoked. Her hands balled into fists, and she slowly stood up. "Did that boy hurt you? If that boy hurt you after I was kind enough to nurse him back to health—"

"No, Mom. He didn't hurt me. I fell in love with him."

"And I suppose that he expects you to follow him back to the nineteenth century just like Jenna and Sarah did.

Is that it?"

"No, Mom. He was all excited about moving *here*. He wanted to go to school and become a lawyer."

"A lawyer? Oh," her mother said, a note of respect in her voice. "It sounds like a fine plan, Madison. So why are you crying?"

"He went to take the GED test—I had signed him up, and he had already studied for it—and he couldn't take it because he didn't have a picture ID." Tears came into Madison's eyes, and soon she was sobbing again.

"Oh. That is too bad. I'm sorry, honey." Kat climbed into the bed beside Madison and put her arms around her. She stroked her hair. "It will be all right."

"I know it will, because I'm going to move back there!" sobbed Madison.

"You're what?" Kat sat up in bed and said, "No! You can't do that!"

"Yes, Mom. It's exactly what I'm going to do. I'm quitting my job and moving to the nineteenth century to be with Zack."

"You're quitting your job? Madison, you can't be serious. What about your career?"

"None of it matters without Zack, Mom. I hate to do it, but Zack's more important to me."

"I knew nothing good would come of that damn cave! First Jenna, then Ryan and Granny, Sarah, and now you. You're throwing your life away for that boy, you know that, don't you?"

"I'm not throwing my life away. I'm living my life. With Zack."

They lay there for a long time like that, cuddled up, with Kat stroking Madison's hair. Madison couldn't remember the last time her mother had cuddled her like this. Maybe it was when she was ten years old, and some bully at school had pushed her down and skinned both of her knees. Instead of going back to class, Madison had run home from school, with her bloody knees dripping. And when she had stepped into the house, she called her mother. Kat had immediately left the office, came straight home to Madison, and cuddled her all night long.

That had been a long time ago. But Madison was an adult now. And as much as she liked the feeling, she knew it would probably be the last time it would ever happen. More likely would be that Madison would be cuddling her own child at some time in the future—or rather, in the past, in the old Red Bluff.

Madison must have fallen asleep in her mother's arms, because next she knew, when Kat stirred, Madison woke up. "I need to get back to work now. But I want you to promise me that you won't quit your job yet. Are you going to work tomorrow?"

"Yes."

"Promise me that you won't give your notice."

"I might as well get it over with, Mom. Nothing is going to change. There's no way for him to get an ID."

"Promise me, Madison. I have an idea. It might work. Promise me that you won't give your notice until I find out if this is feasible. It won't take long. Promise me."

Madison stretched. The short nap had made her feel a little better. "Okay, I promise. What's your idea?"

"I'll let you know if it works. When you get up, email me all the information you have on Zack. Everything you know. Do you have a picture?"

Madison brightened. "Yes! I took one the other night."

"Email me the pic, too. See you later, Sweetie. I'll try my best." Kat kissed Madison on the forehead and disappeared out the door, as silently as she had come in.

CHAPTER FIFTY-NINE

Madison worked extra hard at work Thursday and Friday, because she felt guilty about staying home Wednesday. She kept her word to her mother about not giving notice at her job, but she did start getting her personal belongings together for her move back to the nineteenth century. Although she appreciated her mother trying to help her, she didn't really believe anything could be done. Without breaking the law, getting Zack a birth certificate and an identification card needed a miracle. Madison didn't believe in miracles. She believed in the cold, hard facts. That's why she wanted to become an attorney. Oh well to that one, thought Madison, as she drove home Friday after work.

She parked her car and was surprised when her mother pulled in behind her. Madison waved, opened the door of the house, and waited there. Kat walked up to her with one hand behind her back and a funny expression on her face.

"Let's go in," Kat said.

"What's with you, Mom?" asked Madison.

Kat's eyes were bright with excitement. "I did it,

Madison, I did it!" Madison thought her eyes looked extra bright—like someone who was about to cry.

"Did what?"

Kat pulled her hand from behind her back and handed Madison a manila envelope. On the front it said "Katherine Leyton" and her mother's work address. No one called Kat by her full name, Katherine, unless it was the government. The envelope had a typed notice on it that said "Hand Deliver." Beneath that it said "Attention: Zackary Allen Murphy." It looked official and was time and date stamped in Washington, D.C. "What's this, Mom?"

Kat nodded her head and smiled. "Open it."

Madison opened the envelope and pulled out the contents. There was a birth certificate with Zack's name on it from 1992, with both his parents' names. There was a Diné Tribal Membership Card with his picture on it. And there was a "History Fact Sheet" with information about Zack—most of which was the information she had provided for her mother.

"You did it! How did you do this? Is it legal? Is it real?"

Kat nodded. "Very real. Very legal. I called in a favor from an old friend of your father's. Benny Roth was Billy's best friend in high school. Benny went to college when your father went to war. He was still around for your birth, and he was with me while I gave birth to you. Billy had asked him to do that. We were very close in the months after Billy died."

Madison raised her eyebrows. "How close?"

Kat looked down. "Not that close, Madison, not that it's any of your business! You're my daughter, for cryin' out loud. Anyway, he eventually left Red Bluff for a job in Washington, D.C. I knew he had something to do with the witness protection program, but I hadn't talked to him for years. When I tried to find him a couple of days ago, it turned out that he had been busy these last few years. He worked in the U.S. Marshal's office, and he was *in charge* of the witness protection program. He called in a few favors—especially from the Navajo tribe—and made me swear that Zack wasn't an illegal alien who was wanted in another country, and voila, Zack is now a legal citizen of the United States!"

"I can't believe it, Mom! I can't believe it! You did it! I can still become a lawyer now! And so can Zack! He will be so happy! Thanks so much!" Madison threw her arms around her mother and wouldn't let go.

"You have your paperwork now, and I have to go," said Kat, as she rubbed something out of her eye. "I'm glad it worked out for you. So you'll be heading out there tomorrow to tell Zack?"

"You bet I will," said Madison. "First thing in the morning!"

CHAPTER SIXTY

ZACK HAD SPENT the rest of Wednesday at the bank going through all their pennies, two-cent pieces, and half-dimes. He spent Thursday on dimes and quarters. Friday, he stayed until closing time again, going through all their dollars and half dollars. At the end of Friday, he had found fifty-nine coins that were all worth at least two thousand dollars each. Three or four of them could be worth more than ten thousand dollars.

It was not bad for three days work. If this was to be his job, it wasn't a bad one. He could help Madison with her homework, read the same books, test her—it wasn't exactly being a lawyer, but close. It would have to do until someone figured out a way for him to get a birth certificate legally. Maybe, if he believed long enough that it would happen, then it would. Until that time came, though, he'd have Madison. And for now, that was enough.

Friday, after the bank closed, he went around town and said good-bye to everyone he was close to, saving Matthew and Sarah until last. That one was a difficult and tearful good-bye, but he reassured Matthew by saying that he would see him again—that he'd visit occasionally, and of course he would see them when Matthew and Sarah came to the new Red Bluff to go to the Thai restaurant. Clearly, Matthew was distraught over losing Zack, but at least he had Sarah to help him through. And Zack would be back soon enough. Madison would come back to see Granny before too long, and Zack would come with her. Matthew would be fine.

Zack slept well that night, after packing almost everything in his two backpacks. He was too tired to finish cleaning out his chest of drawers, but he knew he could do it quickly in the morning before he left. He wanted to get out of the saloon before Matthew and Sarah awakened. One teary good-bye was enough.

Early the next morning, as the first rays of light filtered through his curtains, Zack jumped out of bed. He was ready to face the world, ready for his new life. But he still had two drawers to go through. Before Zack had bought the new clothes, he didn't have many possessions. So one drawer was already almost empty. In the back corner, though, was one coin, a half dollar, that must have fallen out of Zack's pants. He picked it up, looked at the date, looked at it again, and then smiled. It was an 1870 CC in excellent condition. Even the shine was still on it. It was worth thousands—many, many thousands. This coin was worth so much that he didn't even need to look at any more for a year!

He put it into the pocket with the fifty-nine coins that he had collected from the bank, and then he opened the last drawer, the one on the bottom. It had some of his father's things in it that Zack had never gone through because it bothered him. His father's death had been hard on him. Now was a good time to go through it since it wasn't daylight yet, and Matthew and Sarah wouldn't be up for an hour or more.

He sat on the bed with a small cigar box filled with his father's belongings. There were only two things in the box: a handmade pipe of his father's that had fresh tobacco in it, as if his father had died before he had a chance to smoke it, and a leather pouch with a rawhide-pull top. Zack opened the pouch and turned it over in his hand. A small piece of quartz fell out along with three coins. Out of habit, Zack looked at the dates before putting them in his pocket.

The first one was a penny; the second one, a quarter; and the third one, a silver dollar. The dates of the first two weren't on his list. The third one, the dollar, was the 1795 silver dollar that Stan had wanted and had called the "Silver Plug." Zack held it to his chest. Stan had said it was "worth a fortune." When Zack had looked it up in his coin book, he found that it had recently been auctioned off for more than a million dollars. With this coin, Zack thought, with this coin, perhaps a million dollars would be enough to buy a legal birth certificate. It was a thought, anyway.

The light coming through the window was getting stronger. He needed to leave before Matthew or Sarah woke up. Zack put the Silver Plug, along with the other sixty coins, into the rawhide bag, closed it, and stuck it into his pocket. After putting the pipe into the outside pocket of the backpack, he quietly walked out the door, down the stairs, and out through the back door, which was closer to the livery. He had settled up with Ezra the day before, so he gave Echo a quick brushing, put on his bridle, hung the two backpacks over a post, and swung up onto Echo's back. Then, grabbing the backpacks, he managed to slip both of them on over his shoulders. He rode out of the livery to his new life.

CHAPTER SIXTY-ONE

EXCEPT FOR THE people who lived in town, Zack wasn't sad about saying good-bye to the old Red Bluff. When he came to the cave, he gave a quick glance over his shoulder, and that was enough. He'd be back. It wouldn't be gone to him forever. And he was so happy with his decision to move to the future even though he couldn't become a lawyer, that only good thoughts floated around in his head. But when he entered the cave and thought he heard the sound of hoofs coming toward him, he motioned for Echo to stop. Maybe someone wanted to steal his coins. That thought almost made him laugh out loud. Who, besides him, knew they were worth anything? But who could it be? Zack had Echo sidestep into the shadows of the cave.

When the person came to the center of the cave where light filtered down from above, Zack saw who it was and couldn't contain himself. "Madison!" he shouted. "Madison!"

"Hi, Zack," she said. "I've got good news for you."

Zack, thinking she was going to tell him that she had decided to move to the old Red Bluff to be with him, said, "And I've got good news for you! I'm moving to your time! I found sixty coins worth a lot of money—we can live in style for at least a year or two! Then, among my father's things, I found the silver dollar that Stan was looking for. He didn't say what it was worth, but it was auctioned last year for more than a million dollars! We're rich!"

Madison smiled and said quietly, "Save your money, Zack. You'll need it for college."

Zack didn't think he heard her right. "What?" he asked.

"I said that you'll need it for college."

"What do you mean?"

Madison reached into the pocket of her cowboy shirt, pulled out a card, and handed it to Zack. "Here. See for yourself."

Zack looked at the card. It had a picture of him on it, and it said "Zackary Allen Murphy, Diné Tribal Membership." "I don't understand," said Zack. He shrugged his shoulders. "This still isn't a birth certificate. Is it enough? Are you sure?"

"There's a whole lot more waiting for you at home—including a birth certificate saying you were born in 1992! Wait until you see it!"

Zack smiled, and although it was difficult hugging Madison with two backpacks pinning back his shoulders, he managed quite nicely. He even kissed her.

"Come on," said Madison. "Let's go home now. I'll tell you everything."

"Can I reschedule the GED test now?"

"As soon as we get home. Boyfriend, you're going to college!"

Zack kissed her again and followed her out the other

end of the cave. Then the two horses walked side by side on the trail, and the humans held hands as Madison told Zack everything that had happened since she saw him last. After Zack told her about his experiences at the bank and then finding the two coins in his chest of drawers, both of them had smiles so big that it hurt their faces.

And Zack, feeling Madison's hand in his own and feeling so grateful at his good fortune, started planning exactly what he was going to buy with all their money. First a laptop, then an iPhone, and of course a small truck would be nice, and . . .

THE END

If you liked this book, sign up on our mailing list to be notified of the next Cowgirls in Time book!
www.RalstonStorePublishing.com/cowgirls.html

In the next Cowgirls in Time romance, read how Kat and Doc discover they have more in common than just medicine.

www.ingramcontent.com/pod-product-compliance
Lightning Source LLC
Chambersburg PA
CBHW061525250926
52052CB00010B/2797
9781938322259